The Sexual Lives of Suburbanites

The Sexual Lives of Suburbanites

A NOVEL IN STORIES

Peter Stenson

JackLeg Press
www.jacklegpress.org

ISBN: 978-1-7375134-5-2

Originally published by Vintage Books, Auckland, New Zealand, 2004.
Second edition published by Blake Publishing, 2006.

Library of Congress Control Number: 9781737513452

Cover design: Jennifer Harris and Jay Snodgrass
Cover art: "The Black Dress" by Turner G. Davis

Contents

The Sexual Lives of Suburbanites

The most impressive aspect of the invitation had to be its actual stock, something sturdy but not overtly stiff, some sort of fortified recycled paper, papyrus maybe. It had a substantial weight for being four-by-four, a nice texture, too. Paul held the invitation in his hand. He gave it a few shakes as if drying a Polaroid. Maybe it was hemp? It was expensive, it had to be, probably bought from a stationary store specializing in custom wedding invitations for matrimonies with Mason jar cups and strung bare bulbs. The only text on the card read *King Tut Party*, followed by an address, date, and time.

Samantha, Paul's wife of thirteen years, asked what he was looking at. He told her the Johnsons were having a party that Friday night.

"Who are the Johnsons?"

"Three houses down."

"Texas Tech bumper sticker?"

"Yup."

"I'd rather..."

Paul enjoyed this part, his wife's habit of conjuring some horrific scenario she would rather endure than partake in a given engagement.

"Use your snoring as a sleep machine."

"Pretty good one."

"A little bit of a reach," Samantha said. She took the invitation from Paul. She rubbed her finger over its textured surface. "Card's nice, though."

"Papyrus, I think."

Samantha fingered the edge of the invitation. Paul knew she wouldn't go. This would incite an argument. He'd hit on the major points of their recent move to Stapleton, Colorado, highlighting their need to give suburban living an actual shot, social functions of paramount importance. She would counter with Stapleton being stupid. Clones on top of clones. She'd say the only reason they'd moved was for their two children's schooling. She would pause, glancing at Paul, almost like she was sorry to have to toss the next insult his way, saying, "And because your parents bought us this house because they deemed the neighborhood safe enough for their precious son."

But Samantha didn't say these things. There was no fight. Instead, she nodded, saying, "I need a night out. Let's do it."

⋮

Friday night rolled around. Paul had been hoping to bump into either Erin or Drew Johnson sometime that week in order to RSVP, and more importantly, ask what constituted appropriate attire for whatever the hell a *King Tut Party* was. This didn't happen. Life was busy with two kids under five. So he exercised logic, settling on khakis and a short-sleeved button-down, casual and understated. Samantha, on the other hand, must've interpreted the invitation differently, emerging from the bedroom in a short black dress, sleeveless, low cut and tight, pumps, a clutch, her hair in a stylized updo. She looked good, really good. Paul felt a stirring he hadn't in a long time. But he also felt as though she'd maybe overdone it a touch. Samantha didn't get out much. This was partially because over the last five years, she'd developed a certain hatred toward people, but also because she'd put her career on hold for the children, often saying if it weren't for dry shampoo, her hair would've been unwashed since Obama's first term. Paul would have to proceed with extreme caution, telling her she looked amazing, but maybe *too* amazing for a low-key summer get together.

"What?" Samantha said.

"You look amazing."

"But?"

"Maybe *too* amazing."

"That had to have sounded less dickish in your head."

"No, what I mean is—"

"You look like a Christian serial rapist. Is that what we're going as tonight? Maybe I should wear something extra frumpy so I can play the part of Unsuspecting Wife of Youth Group Fiddler?"

"What?"

"An invitation that nice calls for something other than your   is-the-fly-of-my-khakis-down-by-accident-or-am-I-fishing outfit."

"What's wrong with my khakis?"

"Nothing. I'm sure the *Johnsons* and everyone else in Stapleton will love them."

The kids were already asleep. They spoke to Mrs. Parker, the only babysitter Samantha trusted, an African American grandma type who'd made a life out of looking after other people's children, telling her they'd be three houses down, their phones were on, shouldn't be out much past eleven.

There was something unglamorous about walking fifty feet to a party. Paul extended his arm; Samantha raised one eyebrow. Paul told her this would be fun. He said she looked beautiful. He added *sexy*, which he regretted as soon as he said it, his face reddening, an admission of trying too hard, of there even being a reason *to* try too hard.

They rang the doorbell.

"I might get kind of shitty tonight," Samantha said.

"Yeah?"

"Might have to. Because I'd rather—"

The door opened. Erin, the hostess, gave a smile perfected on the pageant circuit of the Texas Panhandle. She was attractive in an obvious way—perfume and bone-white teeth and dangling Jarred Heart Collection necklaces nestled between her fake breasts—which is to say Paul had thought about having intercourse with her every time they spoke (as well as every time he stumbled across MILF clips online), but he felt no actual longing for said intercourse.

"The Feinsteins! You look dashing. So glad you two could make it."

Erin hugged Samantha, then Paul. Paul couldn't help closing his eyes when her blond hair brushed against his nose, lost in the citrus goodness of so many high school embarrassments.

They entered the house. It was like theirs, exactly, as in the same model and same color scheme and even the same upgrades in the kitchen—white subway tile as a splash, glass windows in the cabinetry, an oversized granite island—and really, the only foreseeable difference was the odd placement of two dining room tables side by side. Paul didn't recognize anyone. Or rather, he recognized them as people he may have seen while riding bikes with his children or waiting in line at Starbucks, but he didn't know their names. They all seemed to have read the subtext of the invitation regarding dress code (a few tuxes, at the very least a sport coat). Erin introduced them. The next five minutes were lost to the polite shaking of hands and *welcomes* and Paul wondering if anybody would notice if he slipped out to change into something a little nicer. They were given drinks. They downed them with the quickness of the socially anxious. Paul slipped a cheese cube into his mouth. Everyone seemed extraordinarily excited they'd shown up.

If Paul were to list his greatest character assets, small talk would not be among them. He wasn't sure why everything he said to strangers came across as a question. This had gone on his entire life. If he were to venture a guess, it probably related to confidence, a lack thereof, which of course affected the timing of his jokes and witty asides, which made them not at all funny, which made him wonder if people were actually hearing him, which made him speak louder. So that was Paul's small talk, loud barks of mistimed commentary, polite smiles, gulps of wine to hide embarrassment.

Samantha, on the other hand, was a natural. She was quick to smile, quicker to speak her mind, all humor bent on self-deprecation (or the deprecation of those who loved her). People enjoyed her company. When they'd first met in those exciting post-college days, Paul couldn't help but feel that while speaking with Samantha, he was being let in on a juicy secret. It was one of the reasons he'd fallen for her. However, since children, and especially since moving from a slowly gentrifying section of Denver to Stapleton—a proud expanse of flat subdivision, no tree taller than an NBA power forward— Samantha had become more reserved. Paul figured a period of adjustment was in order. But it'd been a month, and Paul couldn't remember the last time she'd left the house without the children. This, of course, had made the initial meet-and-greets with the neighbors difficult, Paul acting as the spokesperson for the Feinstein clan, casting great first impressions of long pauses and shouted jokes.

However, in the span of twenty minutes, Samantha had drunk three glasses of wine, and although she wasn't *shitty*, her mouth was well lubricated, her cocoon of caring for children and DVR'ed TV shows a thing of the past. Paul felt a sense of gratitude at her return to the Land of the Charismatic.

They stood around the kitchen island. Drew, the host, was busy nodding at Samantha, his grin that of every man who loved synthetic golf shirts. They were talking about kids, Drew saying his oldest son had done pretty well with childhood acting—*Have you seen those old E-Trader commercials?*— when Samantha evidently lost interest. She shook her head.

"What's wrong?" Drew asked.

"I'd rather use steel wool as toilet paper than talk about kids on my one night out."

Drew laughed. Paul wasn't in love with how Drew leaned toward Samantha, because he knew that lean, he'd done it (maybe not for a while, a year or two or five, but he'd done it, knowing it was an involuntary reaction to Samantha's magnetism, a physical signal of being let in on a secret).

"You just may be my new favorite couple," Drew said. He stared at Samantha, not even a periphery glance toward Paul.

Paul saw his chance, pouncing with a confident tone: "I'd rather eat that same piece of steel wool than eat one more cheese cube."

Drew cocked his head. Samantha pressed her tongue to the roof of her mouth.

"Sorry if the appetizers aren't to your liking," Drew said.

"No, I like them. I just can't stop eating them, is all I meant."

"With that, I will take my leave. A host's job is never complete."

Drew disappeared into the study. Samantha drained the backwash of her wine. She turned toward her husband. "What the fuck was that?"

"A joke."

"About eating my shitty steel wool?"

"No, about the cheese."

"Why don't we leave the *I'd rathers* to me?"

"Okay."

Samantha appeared to be ready to keep piling it on, but she must've seen vulnerability or at least embarrassment in her husband. She pressed her hand against Paul's stomach. Her breath was soured merlot: "It could've been funny in a different crowd."

"You don't have to say that."

"Will you do me a favor?"

Paul nodded.

"Relax. Drink your wine. Just quit forcing it."

"Sorry."

"Me too," Samantha said. She circled the button on Paul's shirt directly over his navel. "For...you know...everything."

Paul wanted to press her for details, because he took this as an apology for the withdrawing, the anger turned inward, the refusal to give the suburbs a shot. And if there was an apology? Then there was a recognition of the change, meaning there could be improvement, ships being righted, courses set for happier coexistence in the land of neighborhood pools and jogging strollers.

However, as Paul was about to play dumb and ask what she meant, Drew with his marble-statue shoulders told everyone they needed to head to the deck while *preparations were made.*

"Preparations?" Paul whispered.

"It better not be some fucking *icebreaker*," Samantha said. "Because I'd rather donate spinal fluid than do some orchestrated game."

"Nailed it."

"It's coming back," Samantha said. She smiled. She took Paul's hand. He couldn't remember the last time she'd taken his hand.

The backyard was like a diorama of a normal backyard—a wooden deck, tiki torches, a Fischer Price slide, a Weber, a privacy fence stained a little too red—only it was all miniaturized because the backyards of Stapleton were the size of broom closets. There existed a bubbling energy amongst the other guests. Perhaps it was the alcohol? Maybe the *icebreaker*? Hostess Erin rolled her head in circular arcs. One gentleman with a balding ponytail pulled an arm across his body to loosen up his shoulder.

"What's happening?" Paul whispered.

Samantha shrugged. She said, "Maybe three-legged races?"

"Archeologists!"

Paul looked over to the source of the voice. Drew stood on a chair by the door. A few people cheered.

"Welcome to Egypt!"

More cheers.

Samantha said, *Oh fuck.*

"You have spent your entire careers thus far searching for Egyptian treasure. You know it's down there; you have heard rumors of King Tut's tomb; you have developed an obsession with unearthing this god's final resting place."

The guy who'd been stretching his shoulder moved on to some deep lunges.

"Tonight just may be the night you fulfill your life's work and discover the mummified bodies of King Tut and his goddess wife, Ankhesenamun."

"Yeah, it is," Erin shouted. She gave a few high-fives, then turned toward Paul, who put his hand up, more of a defensive maneuver than a show of exuberance.

"You all know the rules," Drew said, still standing on the chair. "Anything goes with the corpses, within reason, of course. Whatever happens with your fellow archeologists is a matter of personal taste."

Samantha turned toward Paul, who shrugged.

"Welcome to the most significant expedition in the world's history," Drew said. He hopped down from the chair and opened the door.

The guests filed in. There was so much yelping. Paul was beyond confused and maybe even a little frightened. However, there wasn't time to discuss those feelings, what with the force of ten or so bodies moving toward the door, he and Samantha caught in a mini stampede.

Inside the kitchen, the lights had been cut. Candles burned on every surface. Not being the tallest of people, Paul wasn't sure what everybody was looking at. It was something on the two dining tables. He figured it was food, something exotic, maybe one of those whole pigs with an apple in its mouth (he'd abandoned his kosher status twenty years upon leaving the Eastern Seaboard, but still...). After a little more jostling, an insurance-salesman type finally moved out of the way. Paul stared at the tables. Two bodies, or what *appeared* to be bodies, lay side by side. They were wrapped in white Ace bandages, head to toe, even the faces. Scratch that; *almost* head to toe, one mummy with bare exposed breasts and a sliver over her crotch, the other bare with a dark, enormous, and painfully stiff penis saluting the ceiling.

Paul rubbed his eyes; there was no way he was seeing this correctly. He turned toward Samantha, who had a hand over her mouth, shocked and horrified, probably a second away from making a scene, calling the police, running home to protect their children, and of course putting the house on the market.

Erin, ever the gracious host, started things off by suckling from an exposed breast of Ankhesenamun. Some sort of didgeridoo-laden trance started playing (evidently, the Johnsons had sprung for the wireless Bose stereo system). Mr. Hamstring Stretcher kissed the female mummy's bandaged mouth. Paul looked around; grins on top of grins. He reached for Samantha's hand, finding it, or maybe it was her hand finding his, hers sweaty and squeezing.

Paul glanced over to his wife. She bobbed and weaved around the elbows and heads of their fellow archeologists. And then she was tugging on Paul's hand. He wasn't so sure what was happening, why his wife was leading him to King Tut. Somebody slapped him on the back. He stood next to the table. Candles flickered. Paul wanted whatever the hell was about to happen to stop, for this night to never have happened, for them to be doing what they did every night, him sitting downstairs watching reruns of *Modern Family* while Samantha hibernated upstairs in their room, the dark glow emanating from their bedroom synonymous with depression. But she was smiling.

Maybe it was the wine and maybe it was the absurdity of a themed orgy and maybe it was a nine-pluser with a curve that Paul figured would only aid in vaginal stimulation, but she was smiling, excited, giddy, a rarity, a teleportation to so many years before.

Samantha stood on her tiptoes. She whispered into Paul's ear: *Touch it.*

Paul assumed she was joking, but alas, she wasn't, not even looking at him for his reaction. Somebody had dipped a hand between Ankhesenamun's legs. *Was the music getting louder?* Paul's carefully selected outfit dampened with perspiration. Samantha squeezed his hand, this time like an excited plea. It wasn't like Paul was homophobic—he'd marched for marriage equality, even had a blue and white shirt with an equal sign on it that he wore on occasion—but that did not mean he was all that comfortable with touching the veiny penis of a man wrapped in Ace bandages while in his new neighbor's home. Samantha's squeezing intensified. She looked up at Paul.

"Please," she said.

"What? Really?"

"I need this. *We* need this."

"You can..."

"I want to watch *you.*"

And just like that, Paul felt called upon. He understood his wife was having a different experience from himself, something not even about an archeologist dig, not even about a penis, but about age and about children and about meal times and mortgages and the compartmentalization of their lives and about no longer being able to shop at certain stores because she'd already worn those styles as a teenager and about becoming people they'd never wanted to be, least of all her, everything about Samantha an active rebellion against the way she had been brought up, the way she now was. And if Paul had to wrestle a python in order to give the only woman he'd ever loved reprieve from their life in suburbia, he would do it.

He understood what he'd always heard women talking about in regards to *girth* when he wrapped his hand around King Tut. He tried to keep his mind scientific, noticing the quick-twitch muscles, the veins, the pulse. Samantha wrapped her hand around Paul's waist. She rubbed his more prominent love handle. Paul stroked. He stroked because Samantha needed him to stroke and because he was finally *cutting loose*, as she'd asked of him, and because he was saving their marriage and because his fellow archeologists cheered him on and never mind the erection he'd sprouted; it wasn't about sex, but about love, for once over the course of their relationship, Samantha leaning into him as if *he* were the charismatic one, his presence a secret other people wanted to hear.

⋮

They left shortly thereafter. The other guests had started to disrobe. Things were being inserted. They hugged Erin on the way out. At the door, she told them Paul's thirty-second HJ had been the sexiest thing she'd ever seen at one of these parties.

Paul and Samantha made love that night. It was the act of their younger selves, but that wasn't even correct; that night they were different people, less restrained. There was no denying what had transpired at the party had changed them, even if momentarily.

Afterward, they lay there struggling for air. Samantha spoke to the ceiling: "Let's never talk about what happened."

"Okay."

"And let's never speak to the Johnsons again."

$$\vdots$$

Things more or less returned to status quo in a few days time. There was work and there was bath time and there was Nickelodeon Jr. and there were chores around the house, even their parcel of yard commanding the better part of a Saturday to maintain. Samantha still went to sleep well before Paul. He would watch shows with easy laughs. He tried not to think about King Tut. He tried to forget about it being one of the most tantalizing experiences of his forty years.

Exactly a week later, Paul found himself alone on the couch. It was nearing ten o'clock; the kids had been asleep for two hours, Samantha one. He attempted to distract himself from the memory of a week prior, so he took out his laptop, hoping to get some early studying on who should be his fantasy football keepers for the upcoming season. He opened Google and started typing in *keeper*, but after the *K*, the dropdown suggestions showed *King Tut Party*. Paul clicked on the option. The first three pages of results showed purple addresses, meaning they'd already been visited. He realized the memories of the party had been with Samantha, as well. But then he noticed the dates the websites had been visited were some ten days prior. This made no sense. Unless...Paul clicked on one of the websites. A picture showed a coed riding a man with what appeared to be papier-mâché wrapped around his body. Samantha had known what a King Tut party consisted of. She'd known and she'd gone along with it. She'd known and she'd played naïve and she'd worn that sexy outfit and she'd probably envisioned Paul masturbating that leviathan the entire time. This realization felt like a betrayal, one he'd been unaware his wife was capable of.

Over the next two weeks, the knowledge of Samantha walking them head-on into a history-themed orgy functioned much like a hatching tapeworm; a larva now born, a slight discomfort, a tickling of his insides, time—each and every minute of his day—acting like a potent growth hormone. He couldn't stop wondering about Samantha's intentions. Why had she taken them to the party? Was she unhappy (obviously she was, but Paul had assumed this was the unhappiness of all reluctant suburbanites, not with...he didn't know...their sex life or his penis or the lack of excitement she experienced seeing him disrobe...)? And if she knew, why hadn't she warned him? And if she was so miserable with their sex life or with *him*, why hadn't she done anything to King Tut?

It was this train of thought that further grew his gnawing worm, it eventually crawling out and down a hole when he started his late night Internet searches. It didn't take long to end up on Craigslist, a personal ad in the *misc. romance* section from a woman who wanted to invite another man into their bedroom so she could watch a male-on-male handie. For some reason, this ad appeased Paul's mind, or rather, it made him feel a little less alone and a lot less like a cuckold. It was a desire, no different from the desire to see his wife make out with another woman. Samantha had researched the party, realized this may be a chance to see her hubby jerk somebody off, which, evidently for her, would be a turn on, and she'd gone ahead with it, knowing that if Paul knew what went down at a King Tut Party, he would balk. In a certain light, this almost made Paul feel good; his wife loved him enough to spark their sex life, all the while keeping things faithful. *Yes*, he would think most nights, dabbing himself clean and exiting the MMF clip he'd been watching, *I think this whole thing has actually been an asset to our marriage.*

$$\vdots$$

The Fourth of July descended upon Stapleton with the force of people who would not be outdone by their neighbors. Flags flew. Potted flowers in patriotic colors spewed from front steps. Grills sizzled. Stereos blared. And of course the place to be was the community pool, which the Feinstein's were, having arrived thirty minutes after opening, thus being relegated to a far corner near the garbage cans, one chair between the four of them.

Paul wore an American flag bathing suit. Samantha took one look at him, shaking her head, going back to applying sunscreen to their youngest.

"What?"

"I'd rather die of an infected cold sore than wear a suit with the American flag on it."

"It's *ironic.*"

"Irony is lost on the suburbs. These people voted for Donald Trump, for fuck's sake."

"Fuck," their youngest muttered.

"That's nice," Paul said. "Come on, let's get in."

"Right behind you, *Captain America.*"

Paul held his children's hands. He sucked in his stomach as he emerged from the asphalt rot of Garbage Corner. His son complained about the concrete burning his feet. A DJ spun top-twenty tunes. Dads wore board shorts like they'd invented them. Moms rocked bikinis that rode an inch below their cesarean scars. Paul smiled and nodded. He was happy to slip into the water so he could relax his gut. Kids screamed. First-time parents hovered; those on their second and third drank spiked lemonades.

"There he is."

Paul turned, seeing Drew, who leaned against the wall of the shallow end. Both of his arms were outstretched like he'd never encountered a more comfortable position. His armpits were shaved.

"Hey Drew," Paul said.

"Happy Independence Day," Drew said.

"Likewise."

"Yup. Our beautiful nation is another year older. I would say *another year wiser,* but I'm afraid two terms of democratic governance has left its mark."

Paul smiled; Samantha had been correct in her assessment of irony in their neighborhood.

"So what have you two been up to?" Drew said.

"Work. Life. The usual."

Paul now stood next to Drew, who turned with a smirk. Drew said, "You been busy jerking off giant Africana cock?"

Paul laughed like this was the most hilarious thing he'd ever heard. His children, thank God, were either drowning or had swum off to the sprinklers. Paul realized he was still laughing, which now sounded psychotic and needed to stop, so he interjected with the first witty thing he could think of: "I wish!"

"No need to yell," Drew said.

"Joking, obviously."

"*Obviously.*"

"That was...whew...crazy night. Cross that off the bucket list," Paul said.

"I'll tell you what I'd like to cross off the bucket list," Drew said. He motioned to the lifeguard still too young for her driver's permit. "You feel me on that one or what?"

"I would love to caress that," Paul responded.

"Bro, show a modicum of volume control."

"Sorry."

"Hey, I'm not the one who's going to be pegged as a pedo."

Again with Paul's ruckus laughter. He scanned the pool for Samantha, a way out of the conversation.

"So what gives?" Drew said. "What's the holdup?"

"Excuse me?"

"When are you guys throwing the next party? It's been like a month. The natives are getting restless."

"I'm not following."

"New guests always throw the next bash. Straight from the swinger's handbook, bro."

"We're not..."

"Says the guy with sticky palms."

"It was a one-time thing."

Drew grinned. He motioned with a flick of his wrist for Paul to come closer. Paul obliged, unsure why he was obeying.

"Listen, I'm not one to give marital advice, but shit, man, did you see how jazzed that little piece of ass you keep locked in your tower was at our soirée?"

Paul felt like he should take offense to what Drew was saying, but he kept nodding like an idiot.

"This is the only way it works, this whole thing," Drew said, waving his hands across the pool. "This whole dream, because that's what it is, don't kid yourself. One giant fucking dream. A dream little girls are programed to want. And we give it to them. And then we both realize it's the most miserable thing in the world. But not if there's an *outlet*. That's the beauty of the parties, man, the rules, the agreements, the parameters. It's the glue that keeps this masterpiece intact. It's the magic fairy dust that affords us the thought that what we're living is actually a dream."

Paul nodded, his mind a thousand miles away, that thousand miles being a few hundred yards, in actuality, the memory of discovering Samantha had known about the swinger's party, had *wanted* to go, had wanted Paul to *cut loose*, had wanted to watch him please another man. And she *had* been happier since that night. This wasn't an enormous spike in the scale, but the trend was upward, the fact she'd agreed to accompany them to the pool a testament to a certain acclimation.

"Plus," Drew said. "I've got a total boner right now looking at all this trim, and if I'm stuck with Erin for too much longer, I'm going on a rampage."

"Well," Paul said. Next to small talk, graceful exits were his largest weakness. "Happy Fourth of July!"

"You too, pal." Drew leaned back into his thrown at the shallow end of the community pool. "Hey Paul."

Paul turned, half his body submerged.

"Remember, magical fairy dust, my friend. A happy wife is a happy life. Don't fool yourself thinking that little HJ's enough to satisfy a woman as sexy as your old lady."

⋮

The thoughts—the facts and near-facts and the fantasies and the justifications and the insecurities—soon took over Paul's life. He'd be sitting with his family. They'd be eating grilled salmon and asparagus. His four-year-old daughter would be describing the plot to the new Pixar film. His two-year-old son would be making truck sounds with his mouth, spit on his food be damned. His wife would be staring off into the depths of her imagination. And he would be telling himself to stay present, to listen to his daughter, to ask his son for the hundredth time to quit spitting, to engage Samantha in something resembling *adult conversation*, but he couldn't do these things, not with his mind twisting in on itself, a horrifying mosaic of living among the Club Eden faithful, his wife's secret plotting, a girthy penis filling his entire hand like he'd never known possible. His tapeworm was nearing adulthood, his insides prone to cramping, his breath always short, a sense of panic so close to the surface. He tried on various affirmations: Samantha is a good wife with swinger tendencies; Samantha knew about the party and went anyway; Samantha liked watching me touch King Tut; Samantha seemed happier then, at least for a few weeks, but that's gone now, the complaints back, the vacancy; Samantha wants to attend another one of those parties, but respects me too much to bring it up; unhappiness always searches for stasis, the most accessible form being the celebration of flesh; Samantha is too strong of a woman to allow depression and the suburbs to confine her; I owe her this, the reprieve from normalcy, the break from matrimony; I am saving my marriage by throwing another party.

He lived the remainder of the summer in the hypothetical. He lost sleep. His appetite shrank, yet he still managed to put on five pounds. He attempted to counter his debilitating thoughts through rededication to his family. He became a mascot of himself or maybe of an ideal. Yet the harder he tried, the more distant Samantha became. One Saturday night (their scheduled copulation evening) in early August, Samantha pretended to be asleep when he walked into their room after putting down the kids. He knew she was faking because she'd taken to cute little snores on the up-beat of her breaths since becoming a mother. Instead of being upset or at least annoyed, Paul felt terrified, suddenly aware that his wife wanted no part of him, at least the part of him he was capable of giving her. It was this instant when he decided to throw a King Tut Party, for if he didn't, Samantha was as good as gone.

So preparations were made. Paul casually ran into Drew, dropping the notion of a party into conversation (blurting it out at an inappropriate volume in the alley as they set out garbage cans). Drew sent over an email list of couples and addresses. Paul did a little research online about the best stationary store in town, finding one in ritzy Cherry Creek, which he visited one day after work. There were so many old ladies inside of the store. Everything looked the same, greeting cards and birthday cards and *sorry I ruined your life* cards. A woman of thirty asked if he needed assistance. Paul asked about postcard invitations, papyrus perhaps. She knew just the one. She asked what he wanted printed. He said *King Tut Party*.

"Umm..." the woman said.

"We're an archeologist group."

"Right."

"I'm serious."

"Whatever."

"Trust me, I'd rather eat shitty steel wool than go to the kind of party you're thinking about."

"What?"

"Nothing. Just these invitations to these addresses, please."

Paul made contact with a catering company. He informed them they would only be needed for setup and cleanup. He booked a spa appointment for Samantha on the day of the party, full mani and pedi and body wrap. He contacted his in-laws, telling them he'd planned a surprise getaway for himself and Samantha, would they mind watching the kids for an evening?

The only thing left to do was find a King Tut and Ankhesenamun. He thought about asking Drew how these selections were made, but part of him felt embarrassed, as if the failure to procure bodies willing to be mummified and fondled was a demerit to Paul's character. So he turned to Craigslist. He spent two days crafting the perfect ad, hitting on gold with the subject line *Needed: King Tut and Ankhesenamun for discreet sensual party.* Within twenty minutes, he'd received forty-five responses. He combed through pictures. He wasn't sure if King Tut needed to be of North African descent, but wanted to be safe, selecting a FWB black couple, the man promising a ten inch penis, the woman promising she was down for anything.

The day of the party, Paul woke Samantha up with breakfast in bed. She gave him a quizzical look, untrusting.

"What?" Paul said. "Can't a guy do something nice for his wife these days?"

"Did you have an accident on the rug?"

"What?"

"Sorry. Gift-horse mouth. Thanks, babe."

Paul set the tray on Samantha's lap. He'd made a rendition of an Egg McMuffin. She asked if the kids were up and Paul smiled.

"What's that smile about? Did you murder them after you shit on the floor?"

"The kids are going away for the night."

"Now you're actually worrying me."

"To your parents."

"What? Why?"

"And you are going to the St. Julian Spa for a relaxing afternoon of pampering."

Samantha's left eye squinted. She said, "If this is you trying to butter me up so I'll have another one of your goddamn kids, you're barking up the wrong tree. I'd rather have a colostomy bag than ever be pregnant again."

Paul laughed. He touched her leg, which felt forced, but a retreat at this point would only make it worse.

"I thought...it'd be nice. For you. A break. For us. You know? A nice, quiet, relaxing evening."

Samantha was about to say something, but stopped, her cutting remark left holstered. She nodded. She took a bite of the homemade Egg McMuffin. She spoke with her mouth full: "Swear to Christ this better not be you trying for Number Three."

⋮

The house was perfect. Paul had spent the better part of the day cleaning and decorating. He'd purchased faux golden cups for the wine. He'd strung lights. He'd taken a collapsible table from the garage and set it next to their dining room table. The caterers arrived at six. He instructed them where to set up the bar and how to stage the appetizers. He had a plastic bag from Target full of every assortment of condom and dental dam made. He cued the Comcast techno channel (no Bose system like the Johnsons, but it would do). At seven, he shooed the caterers out and told them to come back at eleven. He showered, shaved south of the Mason Dixon for the first time in a decade, and dressed in a black suit, even slicking his hair as he'd seen twenty-something's start to do over the past year.

The doorbell rang.

He rushed downstairs, nearly tripping over his daughter's stuffed gorilla, which made him curse, firstly at her lack of care for her belongings, secondly for his stupidity concerning the whole evening; he wasn't the kind of guy who held swinger parties (themed or not); he was in over his head and something was bound to go wrong.

Erin gave him the warmest of hugs. It was that same citrus from her party and from high school. She whispered she couldn't wait to see his cock. Drew gave him an aggressive fist bump. They struggled through guarded conversation, toeing the line between awkward neighbors not about to engage in an archeologist orgy and awkward neighbors *about* to engage in an archeologist orgy. The doorbell rang again. Paul nearly screamed when two African Americans stood outside of his door, the man with all the trappings of rap videos circa '94, the woman with golden earrings, the hoops of which could easily have fit around a softball. There was a long, painfully fearful and racist second of reckoning on Paul's behalf. He finally extended his hand, realizing they were the guests of honor, King Tut and Ankhesenamun. He brought them inside and introduced them to Erin and Drew. Erin offered to help mummify them. The doorbell rang again. Another couple from the list. The ponytailed stretching man waved as he exited his car. It was going to happen; it *was* happening.

Paul pounded two gin and tonics in ten minutes. This did less to loosen his nerves than to loosen the control he had over the volume of his voice. He bounced from group to group, trying to play Gracious Host through the touching of backs and shoulders and cute comments, but he knew he was failing, the stares instead of smiles a difficult to refute hint. He needed Samantha at his side. He needed to be at *her* side. He wished like hell he'd pulled all of the family pictures down from the walls. Where was Samantha? Was the chipotle hummus maybe a bad idea if people were going to be inserting those same fingers in tender orifices? At what point did he shepherd people outside? Did somebody just switch the music to Radio Disney?

"Bro," Drew said. He put his meaty paw on Paul's shoulder. "What say you we get this party started? I took a Cialis an hour ago and I'm ready to rock."

Paul nodded.

He looked around for Samantha. He imagined her getting in an accident, dead somewhere in a ditch off of Highway 36. He thought about her having come home, driving past the house, seeing the festivities through the windows, understanding what was going on because she was smarter than Paul, and her driving away because she wanted no part in it. And then he pictured her sitting in the lobby of the St. Julian Spa and Hotel, all freshly manicured and exfoliated, her ordering a drink, then another, the thought of returning to Stapleton for a forced romantic night with her husband too much to stomach, that second drink now a third, guilt beginning to slip away as she tried on the idea of being a different woman with a different life, this game of make-believe feeling so much better than suburban domestication.

Paul told all of the guests to make their way out to the deck. A few of them cheered. Erin had been in the master bedroom for forty minutes getting the king and queen ready. Paul rushed upstairs with Drew. Two corpses lay on his bed. They were wrapped in bandages. King Tut's penis was simply enormous. Drew and Erin carried down Ankhesenamun. Paul wrapped his arm around King Tut, who jumped a foot at a time. The stairs proved a little easier than the flat carpet. That massive penis made contact with Paul's stomach. He told himself the excitement he felt was from giving his wife her deepest desires.

The door to the garage opened just as Paul and King Tut reached the bottom of the steps. Samantha stood there with her hand over her mouth. Her purse dropped to the floor. Ankhesenamun complained about the table she'd been placed on not being sturdy enough.

"Surprise," Paul said.

Samantha stared at Paul. Her left eye fought against a blink, strained really, shook. She turned and walked back into the garage.

Paul rushed across the kitchen. He jumped down the three steps. Samantha had already started her car. He rushed to the door, opening it as she tried to back away.

"Baby, stop, stop. What's wrong?"

Samantha cried. He couldn't remember the last time he'd seen her cry, at least like this, an ugly cry, one with snot and the contortion of facial muscles.

"I did this for you," he said.

She didn't respond, yanking at the door instead.

"Because you wanted to go. I know you knew what a King Tut party was. I saw the browser history."

She finally quit pulling the door. She looked at Paul. She said, "Are you fucking stupid? The only reason I looked it up was because you came home with the sketchiest invitation in the fucking world. With no postage, mind you. So I thought something was up. I researched a *King Tut Party*. I was disgusted. Fucking disgusted. But I realized it was obviously something you needed to do."

"What are you talking about? I had no idea what it was."

"I realized you needed this for some reason. And you know what? I get it. I fucking get it. I know I'm fucking disgusting since the kids. I know I'm unhappy. I know I can be a cunt."

"I never have thought those things."

"I realized *who could blame you*? Like really? Who could blame you for wanting something like that? So I agreed to go. And then I saw you staring at that dick and I know you're always kind of gay so I gave you your chance. Your *get out of jail free card*."

Samantha recoiled when Paul tried to touch her arm.

"Don't you dare fucking touch me. This...it isn't working."

"It was a misunderstanding. I thought you wanted this. I thought you knew and you wanted me to go and I did this for you, baby, this whole thing for you."

With this comment, Samantha seemed to regain a little composure. She shook her head. "That's the thing with you," she said. "You have absolutely no idea why the fuck you do anything. Marriage. Kids. Your career. Building this stupid fucking house. You do it all like it's a checklist. But who the fuck is keeping score? Who?"

"I do it for you."

"I would rather be with a man who beat me as long as he knew *why* than to be with a man like you who has no goddamn clue why he does a single thing."

"That's not fair," Paul said.

"Here's what's fair, Paul: I give you permission to go inside and do whatever the hell you want. Fuck Erin. Fuck King Tut. Just do something that will *actually* make you happy. Do something for yourself for once in your fucking life. And maybe in the process, you'll develop a shred of personality."

Samantha slammed the door. She peeled out into the alley. Paul stood in his garage surrounded by tools he'd purchased and had never used and clothes his family had outgrown but hadn't yet taken to Goodwill and then the light cut and it was dark and he wondered if they would separate or divorce and if he would be anything without feeling the inclusion of his wife's presence.

Paul made his way back into the house to tell everyone to leave. The lights were cut. Candles flickered. Somebody had righted the channel to some drum-and-bass. Two strangers lay on his tables. Drew had his fingers inside of Ankhesenamun. Erin had her mouth around King Tut. Paul wanted to tell them all to leave. He wanted to tell them all to get a fucking life. To leave his family alone. To go back to whatever pathetic existences they'd shed under the guise of molesting mummified bodies.

But he didn't.

He stood there and imagined himself walking up to his oak table. He'd tap Erin on the shoulder and she'd grin, slobber running down her chin. Paul would stare at the head of a stranger's penis. People would cheer. The music would get louder, maybe switch to some male-led vocals, something melodic and building.

Paul thought about Samantha driving around crying her ugly cries. He thought about the fights they would have later that night or the next day. He wondered if things were beyond repair. If he'd ruined everything. If it was the fault of their kids. If it was Stapleton. If it was the accumulation of shared years. He wondered if it was the end result of a girl settling, firstly with him, secondly in life.

King Tut would moan under Paul's guidance. Somebody would rub Paul's stomach. He'd close his eyes, remembering Samantha doing the same thing to him at the previous party.

He thought about joint custody and he thought about weekends spent with sullen teenagers who wanted to be hanging out with their friends instead of their pathetic father. He thought about sexuality being a continuum and he thought about being gay. He wondered if he'd ever done anything for himself, like *really* for himself, to nourish that inner fraction of soul now occupied by the tapeworm-like gnawing of narcissism and insecurity, or if he'd simply done what was expected of him by his peers and parents and wife. He tried to imagine a different life, one where he was in control, one where he'd quit his job and lived downtown and maybe he'd have sex with women and maybe he'd have sex with men and maybe he'd drink before five o'clock and maybe he'd quit Facebook and fantasy football and golf and maybe he'd even miss child support one month because he'd be that kind of guy.

King Tut's hips would buck.

Paul could do it, change everything, develop a personality. It wasn't too late. Nothing was too late. He could become charming. He could grow charisma. He could attend cocktail parties without buckets of perspiration and volume control handicaps. He could become the person who people wanted to be near. He could become the sharer of intimate secrets.

The hand around his stomach would dip into his pants. The music would strive for a crescendo. Paul would tell himself the hand around his own penis was Samantha's. She would've driven around the block. She would've realized he'd been telling the truth. It'd all been a colossal fuck-up of misunderstanding, but at the heart of the confusion was love for a significant other and the desire to see her happy. Paul would feel the urge to open his eyes and turn toward his wife. He'd beam in her direction. He wouldn't even have to say anything, because she'd know how much he loved her. She'd know he'd stepped outside of himself. She'd know he was working so hard to become a different person, the life of the party, the type of man who took King Tut with his hands because he felt like it.

He imagined leaning into his wife's arms. He imagined her whispering she loved him. He imagined a world in which it was the airing of one's vulnerabilities that functioned as Drew's *magic fairy dust* keeping the illusion of The Dream intact.

Paul turned away from the mummified fornication without saying a word.

⋮

Paul knew Samantha couldn't have gone too far. He drove around the neighborhood, searching for her white Jetta or any sign of movement or really any sign of life. The manicured lawns were vacant. People were safe behind locked doors. There was nothing lonelier than the glow of televisions through drawn curtains. It was no wonder Samantha was miserable here. He realized Stapleton was the last place she'd be. No, Samantha would be in their old neighborhood, the call of the memories of so many of their firsts too strong to resist.

Paul got on the freeway. He called his wife a dozen times, each time sent straight to voicemail. He realized he was crying. But they weren't tears of sorrow, not fully, but of realization and gratitude and *please let me try again*. Because he'd do better this time. He wouldn't force things. He wouldn't be so fucking boring. He wouldn't suffocate. He wouldn't let the children take over every aspect of their lives. He'd take Samantha on dates, once a week, real dates where they maybe drank too much or split a joint or saw a play by some grad school dropouts. But most importantly, he'd squash the distance that had grown between them. He'd never let her fall asleep while he watched TV downstairs. He'd never let them become strangers enough to engage in King Tut parties out of a complete lack of understanding about the other's wants.

He exited the highway. He drove through an older part of town, still predominantly Hispanic, the schools rated among the worst in Colorado, their old neighborhood, what still felt like home. Paul knew Samantha would be at Cesar Chavez Park. That had been their haven, their sanctuary, a stretch of grass and playground that had been the constant of their lives for a decade. Samantha had even once joked about being buried there. Of course she would be there; it was the tableau of her happiest moments as a young woman and wife and new mother.

Paul parked. He rushed out of the car. The city had evidently paid heed to complaints, adding a few lampposts to deter drunks and assaults. He jogged up the stairs. He scanned the playing fields for movement. He ran out thirty yards before realizing she would be on the playground. His heart soared when he saw a shadow on the teeter-totter. He sprinted. Of course she was on the teeter-totter. She'd spent hours upon hours on that very piece of splintery wood with their daughter. Up and down, up and down, every time Samantha laughing beautiful laughs, free.

He slowed down at the start of the woodchips. He tried to catch his breath. Samantha faced the other way. He needed his words to be perfect. He needed to once in his life say the right thing at the right time at the right decibel.

The words came to him without a second thought: "Samantha, I get it. I do. We had everything. We were happy. *You* were happy. *I* was happy. I'm sorry I took that away from you. Please give me another chance for us to get back to how we were."

Samantha turned around.

Only it wasn't Samantha, but some girl, a teenager with dreadlocks in a hooded sweatshirt. She frowned. She said, "Sorry man, not Samantha. But even if I were, that shit there wouldn't matter. The saddest thing in the world is nostalgia for the sake of love."

The girl slipped off the teeter-totter. She nodded and headed toward the street.

Paul scanned the playground. He was alone. Samantha was nowhere to be found. It didn't make sense; Samantha would be *here*. Maybe that was true of the woman she'd been. But the woman she was now? Paul hadn't the faintest idea where his wife would be. Not even a clue.

You May Know Me as The E-Trader Baby

You may know me as the E-Trader Baby—the phenom that is the stock-talking infant from the commercials—but the name's Thurman Johnson. I know, *Thurman*. Thanks, Dad, like sorry I turned out white and not linebacker-sized. But whatever, play the hand you're dealt. And that's what I keep telling myself lately: *Play the hand you're dealt.* It's a stupid cliché, something my dad's been saying my entire twenty-four months on this earth, because he's just that type of guy, the kind who embraces clichés as a kind of worldview, but I find it apt at this particular time, nonetheless. You see, things aren't exactly warm milk and perfect burps right now. In fact, in my estimation, my current situation is basically three not-so-great things:

1) Thermo-Ozone Research, LLC (TOR)—Pretty much a can't-miss startup coming out of Cambridge, like two Harvard kids whose sole purpose for existence was to create a false ozone through the selective heating and cooling of water vapor, essentially tricking the oxygen molecules to jump ship and bond in nice little groupings of three. The concept was brilliant, the specs perfect. It just didn't work. Not even a little bit. So that was everything I had, 45K, plus a hardy 10K from Michelle, which brings me to the second crappy thing in my life:

2) Michelle—You probably remember things were a little rocky with Michelle from that commercial a year ago. First off, it was horrible of my parents to be filming that, like we'd had the agreement that my play dates were exactly that, *mine.* But they kept the feed running. So when Ellie was over—nothing was even happening, just kicking it in my crib— Michelle Skypes, gets mad, and then a month later, her embarrassment is broadcast into every home in America during the Super Bowl with a fricking 43 rating! Jesus, can you imagine? But I got it smoothed over because I'm good like that and really, I love Michelle, those cheeks like the fattest of milk sacks, like you can tell Mrs. Hendricks breastfed well into eighteen months, unlike my mom, who cut me off after six, but that's a different story. But what's important is that things were finally good again, Michelle-wise, and then I convince her to dump all the money she made from appearing in that embarrassing commercial into Thermo-Ozone Research. And well, that's 10K she'll never be getting back. The last thing she said to me two weeks ago was, *Make it right, or we're done,* which brings me to bummer number three:

3) E-Trader is done with me—*Fin. Finis.* Don't call, don't text, don't Skype. Thanks for coming. The suits didn't even have the decency to inform me of

this decision in person. They did it over mail, *postal* for God's sake. It was such BS, like something about *a child nearing twenty-four months with the ability to talk is not uncommon.* Like can you believe that? Sorry I'm getting older. That's what happens. How many other two-year-olds do you know capable of managing funds and creating portfolios that would make Buffett cream his pleated khakis? I still think I have a skillset most don't. Christ. So I'm washed up. Sweet. Two years old and washed up. Done in the entertainment business. And my little nest egg is squashed, thanks to those dweeby kids from Harvard, and Michelle won't talk to me. Washed-up, broke, and single. This is my life.

⋮

So I'm at the dinner table, sitting in my Deluxe Toddler Throne II, a relic from a more decadent time, eating what can barely pass as bits of scorched chicken breast. I'm thinking that my mom is the worst cook ever, that I was better off eating puréed haricot verts from Gerber, and I'm wondering how much longer this will be my life, the eating of food unfit for death row inmates.

"Eat your chicken, Thurm."

I give her a smile, sly, the one America used to love. She takes this as a sign of encouragement. She mauls a piece of my chicken in her sausage fingers and airplanes it toward me and it's so damn demeaning, the buzzing sound she makes, but it always works, because it's like the chicken *is* a plane. I chomp it down.

"How was your day, honey?" my mom asks across the table.

My dad is silent for a second. This is not like him. I glance over and he's looking at his chicken and I'm thinking oh, goodie, this is the moment he snaps, says what we're both thinking, *This chicken is horrendous,* but he doesn't. He just says, "They laid off another fifteen people."

"You didn't—"

"No, I'm fine. For now."

"Baby."

This endearment makes me jealous.

"Henry, Pam, Jorge," my dad says.

"God, *Jorge?*"

Dad nods. The little blood blister thing above his eye turns a little darker, crimson maybe. He pokes at his meal. I'm thinking that maybe he wants Mom to give him the airplane, and this makes me laugh, and they both turn, and then I feel like a jerk.

"But they're done now, right? I mean, they can't keep laying people off. Nobody will be left," my mom says. She finishes her chardonnay. I'm pretty sure it's her second glass—no, third, she had one while cooking dinner—and it's becoming something of a habit, this drinking. I think about bringing up the fact that the occasional picking of my nose is far less harmful than this newfound love of wine.

"They said more could be expected at the end of the quarter."

"What?"

My dad's not looking at anything. I'm looking at him and it's embarrassing, he is, this fear, and I want to tell him to *play the hand you're dealt*, and his growth or whatever, it's getting even darker, past the spectrum of red and onto shades of purple. I try to remember where I've seen that before, that color of purple of his bump, and then it hits me: two Saturdays ago, when Michelle was supposed to come over for our weekly play date, and my dad told me that Michelle was still sick and wouldn't be coming over, and I knew he was lying straight to my face, and his little blister thing was so full of blood it was like Barney. And then I was like OM-fucking-G, he's lying. Right now. Sitting there trying to stomach this disgusting food, he's lying. He got laid off too.

"I don't know," he says.

"But you're okay, right?"

He nods again. Maybe he knows his voice will betray him so this is all he can muster. A continuous nod's as good as he can do, his pinky nail-sized blister nearly black.

$$\vdots$$

Later that night in my crib, I'm pretty much rock-bottom-down. I crap my pants and don't even fuss. I just lie there staring at the animals painted on my wall—giraffes, elephants, smiling lions, an out-of-place wolf or coyote—thinking about my mother two years before being so excited to paint a mural for the son in her stomach, finally using that art education background for good use. I think about my dad and his lies, but who could blame him? Like what, he comes home and says, "We're screwed. We're going to lose the house. Sorry, hon, I failed!" I picture all of us packing up the house and my mom putting my toys in boxes and looking at the mural that probably signified love and safety and the start of a family, theirs, and I'm cussing those unprofessional dicks from Thermo-Ozone Research and then it's Michelle's cheeks, like the object of affection of every motherfucker on the block, and then I realize that my *making it right*, like she said, isn't just about her. It's about everything. And if I could scrounge up a decent amount of capital, I could do it, hit on some penny stock in Bangladesh, and then my dad wouldn't have to worry about the implications of being fired and my mom wouldn't continue the escalation of glasses drunk and Michelle would hear about this, how I saved the GD family, and she'd take me back.

I formulate a plan. Then I'm starting to itch, the contents of my diaper drying, so I let out a few wails.

⋮

I'm in the breakfast nook when my dad comes in. He's dressed in his suit and he kisses me on the top of my head and this busts me up a little bit, both because he always said my hair smelled like heaven and because he's going to drive around for eight hours pretending to be at work.

"See you, Pops."

"Love you, Kid-O."

I mow through my Cheerios. I need my energy because I have a full day ahead of me. I look at the first step on the list I wrote-up last night:

1)   Find can't-miss penny

We've come up with an agreement, Mom and I. I get two hours on the computer a day. *Two hours*, that's it. Like really, what can I get done with that? That's barely time to update my status. It's just that once the E-Trader commercials aired, she started getting hate mail telling her bad mother this, negligent exploiter that. I guess she started believing it, so ground rules were established. Two hours. No more, sometimes less.

Luckily for me, my boy, Brock, owes me big-time, say to the tune of sixty-seven large, for my heads-up on shorting GM last year. I send him over a message: *Bro, need a sure-thing penny.*

A few minutes later, Brock replies with some convoluted message, obviously giddy with the reversal of power. He tells me about a small Indian company, Shimla Pharmaceuticals. He says they put out a cure for gout, but since gout isn't much of a concern in India, it hasn't blown up yet. The kicker, Brock writes, is that Shimla Pharmies is rumored to be attending the New York Pharmacological Expo starting on Wednesday; *it's a matter of days until the rich white guys in America discover the pill, buy it in bulk to cure their nasty toes.* I've never much trusted pharmaceuticals, especially those companies from small Indian provinces, but desperate times call for desperate measures.

God, I'm so my father's son with these clichés.

I look up the company on the Bombay Stock Exchange. They're trading for roughly the equivalent of six cents a share. A little pricy, but it could be the one. Normally, I spend weeks pouring over the smallest of investments, but there's not time. If Brock is right, which I only kind of suspect he is, the NYC Expo is in two days, and now would be the time. The BSE shows the latest sale jumping .5 cents. I'm thinking I need to work fast, fortunes aren't won by the cautious. I tell myself to think about Thermo-Ozone Research, how long I tracked them, practically from senior thesis to first public offerings, and how this didn't help. I send Brock one last message: *u sure?*

He writes: *positive as a pregnancy test.*

I cross number one off my list.

I've got a little time left so I see if Michelle is online. I shoot over a Skype. I'm thinking about Michelle, the most perfect person in the world, how her giggle always trailed upward at the end of a good laugh, how the term "girlfriend" was a blasphemous characterization of what she was to me because we were so much more than that, the two of us best friends, frickin' soulmates, equally happy to be watching Baby First as we were nibbing on one another's earlobes. The Skype call rings and rings and rings.

2) Procure the funds.

I suppose this is the problem with any thievery—the *how to.* Of course everyone knows banks house money and museums art and stores jewelry, but that doesn't help. It's how to get in there and steal it, all the while leaving no trace behind. My bank is the top drawer of my father's white built-in dresser, the thin one where he stashes his tighty-whities and emergency credit card. I know this because I saw him put it there a month ago, right after mom came home with yet another set of dishware, these ones Fiesta, orange and fairly hideous. I had been sitting on the floor of their changing room. I could hear them arguing—*Jesus, Erin, more dishes?*—*We needed an autumn set*—*Give it over, the card*—*No*—*Erin, now.* My dad had come walking back into the dressing room. He'd exhaled quite dramatically, then smiled at me. He'd slid the card behind his underwear.

So that's my Louvre, the credit card my Mona Lisa.

But currently, I find myself stuck in the pen, as in *playpen*, as in walls higher than my hands can even reach. My mom scurries around the kitchen. She does this a lot, *scurrying*, busywork I guess. It seems her entire day is a practice in kinetic energy. Like maybe she feels worthless about being home since my arrival, not working anymore, and the only way to combat those feelings of uselessness is to scrub every surface with antibacterial aerosols. What I'm telling you is that she's a worthy opponent, a continuously moving guard. I need her to relax. I need her to sit and kick up her feet so I can make my escape and retrieve the credit card. I need her to start drinking.

I start to cry. This is easy enough. I start faking it and then I think of Michelle not answering my calls and then my acting gets better. Mom comes over, all blonde hair poking out from her scrunchy.

"Thurm, don't tell me you..." She grabs the back of my Snuggies—not *diapers*, mind you, I've been off those for two months, but *pull-ups*, for *big boys*—and she takes a look at my backside. It's clean. I cry harder. She says, "What is it?"

I give her my best pout, let the edges of my mouth shake a bit, and it's like I can't even get the words out, my acting, my baby carrot fingers rubbing my eyes. I say, "I'm worried about Dad."

This works. She pulls me out of my prison and brings me to her stomach. I bury my face in her neck. I love the smell of my mom, the Clinique citrus of her body-wash mixed with the powder fresh of her Sure and then it's the quintessential *Mom*, that sweat or breath or something. She's patting my back and telling me, *Shh, it's okay, shh.*

"He's fine, Thrum. You heard him last night."

I play it up. I say, "What about Uncle Jorge?" (He's not really my uncle, but people without children love when they're given this prefix.)

My mom catches on an inhale. She keeps rubbing my back. I'm loving it. "I know, it's tough out there, you know that."

And then I let loose. I need to. I need to catalyze her percolating fears, the ones she pretends aren't there, the ones that are the source of her every passive aggressive comment: the fear of losing everything. The life. The ease. The stuff. The pride that comes from climbing social cliques like the wooden steps of a playground, of bettering themselves, of working their way from one class to another, middle to upper-middle with all our Stapleton neighbors.

I whisper, "We're going to have to sell the house."

"No, Thurm, we'll be okay."

I'm shaking my head. I'm not proud of this, my fear mongering, but it's all for a greater cause, to save this family from the economy and the country and from itself, so I keep going: "Dad's going to lose his job like Uncle Jorge. And then we'll have to live with Grandpa Bob and Grandma Emmy."

I can tell it's working because my mom quits rubbing my back. This means her mind's spinning with thoughts of financial destitution and nightly meals eaten with her parents.

"It's going to be fine."

"Where will I sleep?"

"What?"

"At Grandma Emmy's? They only have one spare room."

This does the trick. She turns away from me. I keep telling myself it's what needs to be done, this fear abuse, that I need her to be beyond distracted, for her to find solace in a fresh bottle of white wine. She's so close. I push harder. "The third quarter ends in two weeks. Dad said that's when they would fire more people."

"Jesus," Mom says. This isn't a word that normally escapes her mouth. She's pacing. She's bouncing me and I try to keep focused on the goal, but the rhythmic jostling is so soothing—*Focus, Thurman, almost there*—so I tell her that I want some juice.

This is of course in order to get her into the kitchen. She sets me on the counter. I like the way the granite feels on the backs of my thighs. She reaches to the shelf for my sippy cup.

This is my moment. I need to seal the deal. I need to close, close, close, and I'm thinking about my idols, the Trumps and Buffetts and Gordon Gekkos of the world, the men who seized opportunity, disregarded everything else, and that's who I'd wanted to be since my first trade, since I stumbled across my father's E-Trader account and clicked ten shares of Apple (when it was still sub-century mark), and I think about how my father had been sleeping on Apple, how he championed the theory that the iPhone would never make a dent, and I think about him trying to navigate this century with an outdated vocabulary and mindset. I picture him sitting at Hidden Falls Monument eating a Subway six-inch, an Italian melt, him trying to summon the courage to tell my mom about being fired. Mom's at the refrigerator. And it's *playing the hand you're dealt* and it's for the common good of the household and for Michelle and I say it: "They have no use for aging analysts."

She pauses. I'm staring at her arm, its top, her tri, how it sags like a hammock despite the exercise classes. It will never again be flush with her bone. This is the price of bearing children and making it into one's mid-thirties and drinking wine. Her hay-colored hair starts to shake. Maybe I'm a bad person. Then it's more than her hair shaking, but everything. I'm looking at the back of her arm swaying and this is the most human thing I've ever seen.

She doesn't say anything.

She fills my cup, the blue one.

Then she fills a wine glass, the big one.

⋮

I don't need to worry about my mom tracking me. She's pulled the red throw around her knees and ankles in the leather easy chair. She's holding her wine like hot chocolate, two hands around the cup, its rim inches from her mouth, the faintest of lipstick kisses speckling its outer edge.

And when I push the sitting chair in their dressing room over to the drawers, I keep telling myself it has to be done.

And when I rush back to the study, credit card in hand, I tell myself I'm saving the family.

And when I max-out the card for twenty-large on Shimla Pharmaceuticals at 6.5 cents a pop, purchasing 307,692 shares, I tell myself that gurgle in my stomach is from the apple juice, not from spending the last of what our family has access to.

I'm shaking when I cross off number two from my list.

I'm not into the next step:

3) Wait.

⋮

At dinner that night—Tater Tot hotdish, a personal favorite of mine—we're all quiet and civil and eating with our heads down. My mom drinks a glass of water. Her breath is the bath of mouthwash she'd taken before my dad got home. I wonder if she's fooling anyone. My dad, he's in his suit, the tie loosened two inches. He's taking the bites off his fork with his teeth. It's enamel on sterling silver. He tells us the office was down today, fearful. I wonder if he's fooling anyone. And I'm smushing Tater Tots because that's what I do, what is expected of me, and I kind of love doing it, because their insides are perfect squares, which makes me normally giggle, but I'm not tonight, giggling that is. I'm just crushing them, then eating the individual squares one at a time. I wonder if I'm fooling anyone.

For some reason I think about Michelle. I picture her sitting in her highchair, Mrs. Hendricks at one end, Mr. Hendricks the other. Maybe they're having the same hotdish. Maybe Mrs. Hendricks is pretending to be fine with water and Mr. Hendricks is pretending that their livelihood is as secure as WWII Bonds. And then I'm thinking about everyone I know, all of my friends from playgroup, all of their friends and distant cousins and then theirs, everyone, a supernova spreading out from Denver to Chicago to Cleveland to Philly to New York, the same thing westward, all of us eating the same meal, all of us pretending the status quo isn't crumbling the fuck apart beneath our ARM-ed homes, all of us convincing ourselves that this status quo is still a worthy thing to be pursuing.

$$\vdots$$

I sneak a quick glance at the BSE between bath-time and bedtime. Shimla's latest trade was at 10 cents. I give a quick *hell yeah* and run off to bed.

They come in separately, which is new over the last month. First my mom. She comes in and I'm kind of in the mood for a story and I tell her this. Her breath of Scope and wine reach me first: "Not tonight, honey, not tonight."

Then it's kisses on my nose and this makes me coo.

"Love you, Mom."

"Love you, too."

Then it's my dad, maybe fifteen minutes later. For some reason, I pretend to be asleep. I face the wall. I can feel him standing there. He just keeps standing there. I make my breathing louder to really convey that I'm conked out. He still stands there. He sniffles. Again. I give a fake spasm in my left leg. Then it's the muffled sound of him crying and I close my eyes even harder and I remember the one time I'd seen him cry, maybe a year ago when he got off the phone with his mother, when she'd told him that his father was diagnosed with stage 3A prostate cancer, inoperable. I'd been playing with a stuffed block set on the floor. I'd stopped, looked at him, my father, indestructible, never even a question. He hadn't hung up the phone, but instead held it in his lap. Then it was the tears and he bit his lip with such force I worried about it bleeding and then it was the phone beeping from being off the hook—long, eerie wails throughout the dusk-lit house.

$$\vdots$$

I nearly crap my Snuggies the next morning when I see the price of Shimla Pharmaceuticals is at 20 cents a share. And when I say *nearly*, I mean *actually*. I can't believe it. I do the math on a piece of scratch paper:

$307,692 (shares) X $0.2 = $61,538.4

$61,538.4 - $21,400 (twenty grand plus 7% cash-advance surcharge) = $40,138.4

I Skype Michelle. She doesn't pick up. I IM her. No response. Same with G Chat. I know my *making it right* isn't words, but instead actions, which leads me to the fourth thing on my list. I pull the scratch paper out of the waistband of my Diego pull-ups.

4) Get my baby back

I sell 60,000 shares of Shimla. This nets me twelve K, which I deposit into Michelle's PayPal account with a memo—*hope this makes it right*—and that feels too snarky so I try again—*here's what I owe you plus interest*—and that feels too formal so I think about the first time we ever held hands, us barely out of the hospital, us just amorphous slobbering blobs laying on a shared fleece blanket, me noticing this absolute drop-dead gorgeous looker for the first time, venturing my nubs of fingers over to hers, and then that moment when she looked—God, those milk-sack cheeks!—the glint of a promise in those watery brown eyes, and her Barbie-sized fingers grasping mine. I start tearing up because she means more to me than anything. I'd been so stupid ever agreeing to the play date with Bethany. I see that now.

I write this in the memo: *I love you more than anything. I hope you know that.*

⋮

That afternoon, I'm taking a snooze in the Pack-N-Play. Mom's cleaning again. Dad is probably sitting at the park in his suit. That's when the doorbell rings. I open one eye and watch my mom scurry over to the door. I can hear her saying things like *wow* and *my goodness* and *thank you*.

This gets my attention. I climb up and rest my forehead against the mesh netting of the crib. She comes back in with a bouquet of flowers—a modest autumn-themed collection of irises and stars of Bethlehem.

"Somebody loves ya," I say.

My mom laughs. She walks over to the crib. She sets the flowers on the shelf next to the TV.

I figure this is Dad's way of lessening the blow, first peppering her with flowers and love, then delivering the news.

"Let's just see," my mom says. She pulls the little card out from the center of the bouquet. She reads, "We have no doubt you'll land on your feet. Work isn't the same without you. With much love, The Office."

My mind is *no, no, no.* I need to think fast. So I laugh, like really loud, slapping my thigh like I'd seen my dad do watching reruns of *Cheers.* I say, "Those guys are such tricksters."

My mom doesn't look at me, but instead at the card, light purple cardboard in her manicured fingers. Her lips move as she rereads.

"It's a *joke*, Mom."

She doesn't say anything, just turns and walks to the kitchen. She pauses with the cordless in her hand. My mom with her flabby triceps, my mom debating if she could do it. Then she sets the receiver back in the cradle and goes to the fridge. A sight that filled me with joy just a day ago—the uncorking of white wine—now today feels horrible. She fills the glass. She doesn't place the bottle back in the fridge.

I want to tell her not to worry, we are forty thousand richer since last night, Dad will bounce back, and even if he doesn't, I can take care of us all. I am smarter than him and understand the markets and it will be okay, all of us, our mortgage at eight-and-a-half points, we won't have to move in with her parents, it will all work out, it always does, we'll get through the worst of it.

But I don't tell her anything.

I just watch her refill her goblet.

And then yet again.

⋮

Dinner is ready when my dad gets home (chicken tetrazzini, dry like you wouldn't even believe). Dad pecks my mom on the cheek, then the top of my head. He looks haggard, as if his front is maybe more tiring than actually working. I sneak his Blackberry from his suit jacket and check Shimla: 32 cents a share. We're rolling in the money, and if my boy, Brock, is right, like it's looking like he is, and a company like Pfizer swallows up Shimla at the NYC Expo, we could be looking at a cool million.

My dad says grace.

My mom isn't masking her drinking tonight. She takes a gulp before my dad mutters *amen*.

I'm nervous about their bubbling confrontation.

She serves us. My dad says, "Looks great, hon."

She gives him something resembling a smile.

I want to warn him. To tell him she knows, that whatever excuse he's planning is futile, worthless, will only dig his grave deeper. I glance over at my mom. She's topping off her chardonnay, staring at my father. She's flexed, like her whole body, and it's menacing, the quiet calm of her movements.

"So, sure was nice today," I say.

"Yeah. Looked that way," my dad says. He stomachs what is in his mouth. "Wouldn't really know, though."

My mom sees her chance and jumps in: "Why is that?"

"Hope it stays this way," I say.

"Why is what, honey?"

"That you wouldn't know?"

I'm trying my best to diffuse the situation, to change the subject, deflect her inquisitions, so I say, "I saw that tomorrow was supposed to be just as sunny. High of sixty-five. Can you believe it? Sixty-five in early November?"

"What is that supposed to mean?" my dad asks.

"Just uncommonly warm for so late—"

"What do you think it means, Drew?" my mom says.

I know nothing I do will stop the barreling trains of my parents. I am Baby, even though I have the better mental capacities than either of them, and this means I am not to be part of Grownup Conversation.

"I don't know," my dad says. He wipes his mouth with an orange cloth napkin, ones that match the orange Fiesta ware. "Why don't you quit speaking in code, and tell me what you're getting at?"

My mom snorts. She drinks. She looks at her food, then at my father, straight into his eyes. She says, "Why are you lying?'

My dad shakes his head, feigning bewilderment. "What are you talking about?"

"Seriously?"

"Erin, I have no—"

"Jesus Chri—" She stops, looks over at me, before continuing in a quieter, yet harsher tone: "Don't you dare sit there and lie straight to my face."

My dad leans back in his chair. His blood blister has turned purple. I'm thinking this is probably the time when I should tell them about Shimla and of course they'll be angry I stole the credit card, but that's okay because it will diffuse the situation, and underneath that expected parental anger will be joy at the income, at me saving the family. So I say, "I have something to tell you guys."

"I haven't lied," Dad says.

And then my mom's crying. She's trying not to, but she is, I can tell, the way she flutters her eyes like they need air.

"So, I went ahead and made a little investment..."

My mom's glass is empty.

My dad fingers his ring.

"Who do you think I am? Honestly, Drew? That I wouldn't understand? Like what kind of person do you think I am?"

The tears lose their balance and tumble down her face.

"Shimla Pharmaceuticals, and it's doing very well, like I've made an enormous amount of money..."

"Erin, I don't know what you're—"

And then it's my mom pushing back her chair, throwing her napkin over her plate, and I'm wondering why the hell he doesn't come clean? Like how hard is it? Like he was backed into the tightest of corners, no way out, and then I'm thinking about when I had to tell Michelle about Thermo-Ozone and how this was over Skype and she just stared at me and it wasn't love in those eyes, but, God, I don't know, *pity* maybe?

My mom stands with her hands on the back of the mahogany chair. "The one thing that I thought we still had was trust." She doesn't bother with the bubble of snot bull frogging out of her right nostril. "But I see we've lost that, too."

⋮

I don't get a bath that night. Mom's locked herself in her room and Dad's walking around the neighborhood. So I climb into his leather office chair. Shima's latest trade is 39 cents. I'm rich. I want to share this with somebody, anybody. Michelle isn't online. Probably getting a bath. Or maybe Mr. Hendricks is out walking around the neighborhood because he was laid off too. I picture Dad and Mr. Hendricks crossing paths and I wonder if they would stop to talk or just keep going after a silent nodding of heads. None of my friends are available on G Chat. I keep hitting refresh, refresh. And I'm thinking about my mom and dad and if he'll come clean and tell the truth when he returns from his walk. I wonder if she'll be forgiving, take him in her arms, kiss his swollen eyes, tell him she understands he is trying the best he can.

Refresh.

I just want Michelle to say that she forgives me. That she knew nothing was going on with Ellie and that she knew I could get her money back and provide, that's what she'd say, *provide*, and I'd tell her *damn right* and we'd laugh at this, us together over fiber optic cables, us together in knowing we'd never lose our house. We'd be better than our parents, better than theirs, and on back down the line to our ancestors fleeing protestant persecution and landing on this little can't-miss piece of land. Better than them all. And I'd tell Michelle she could buy whatever dishes she wanted, ugly orange ones even.

Refresh.

I hear the backdoor open. I strain my ears, waiting for my father to come lumbering up the stairs. But he doesn't. I hear what sounds like the closet door. Then I hear the TV. And then I understand he's retreated to the living room couch and isn't even going to try and this breaks my fucking heart because it's only pride. I want to yell at him, tell him to *try,* goddamn it, to apologize. Shima sells for 42 cents. I hit refresh. And I will not be my father with his Old World views and I will not be my mother with her silent resentment and I will not be their generation because I will not lose everything I've worked for. Shima climbs over 45 cents a share. Everything will work out, Michelle and I. Refresh. I'll amass more than ever can be lost. I want to tell my father to get it together, to *pull himself up by his bootstraps,* to *play the hand he's dealt*—47 cents, refresh— and I want to tell him to believe in the shit he's been spouting since I was born.

The only light in the study is the white humming of the monitor. I switch between screens. The desktop is a picture of all of us—Mom and Dad and myself—and it's a selfie taken in the backyard just this past summer. It was my first foray into watermelon. My face is covered and this had made them laugh, my parents holding me in their laps, their faces covered too, little bits of pulpy flesh circling our mouths, smiles, things still okay then.

I want my mom to read me a story. I want my dad to kiss my hair. I want Michelle to accept my apology.

I go to YouTube and watch my commercials.

I'll be a millionaire in the morning.

Refresh.

Refresh.

A Night in Ten Frames

Sandy Casoli loved the Bravo Network and Sudoku and was only so-so into bowling, but that's where she was, Split This!, a twenty-lane alley, each and every lane occupied. She stood next to the ball dispenser. She held a ball, pink, but ugly pink, too soft, too washed out. Her husband, Daniel, told her to line it up with the arrows. She didn't acknowledge this with anything but the bobbing of her black ponytail. *Line it up with the arrows,* she mocked inside of her head. Dick. She listened to his voice, the way it had started to become deeper around other people. He was giving encouragement and bits of advice and then it was comments about her taking all night and this, of course, was followed by a rip-roaring laugh, fake, a show, look-at-me-I'm-Funny-Husband, and sometimes, Sandy knew his newly sober pep-talks and smothering glances were because he loved her, but tonight wasn't one of those times.

She walked over to the lane. She didn't look at the arrows. She looked at the pins. She heaved the ball. It was heavier than she remembered. It started down the middle and veered a little to the left. All but one pin fell.

Clapping from behind her and Sandy turned and Daniel was giving her a thumbs-up and Becca smiled her born-blonde smile and Jorge nodded. Sandy said, "See, girl's got game."

Daniel said, "It was great, baby, now just aim a little further over."

Sandy's ball burped out of the retriever. She picked it up. She inserted her fingers. She thought about getting the last pin down and the big to-do Daniel would make out of a strike or spare or whatever the hell it was called and then she thought about the reason Daniel had been pushing this double so hard—her sobriety, wanting some of Becca to rub off on her, the cork in the jug, Twelve Steps, for Sandy to experience some of the *joy of living* as Daniel had started calling it over the last eighteen-months of his non-drinking—and Sandy didn't aim, just walked and heaved, thinking it was such bullshit, her husband's sobriety, him changing the rules halfway through their lives.

The final pin fell.

⋮

Jorge Rodriguez looked more black than Hispanic and had been dubbed Thunder Stick during his one semester as an Alpha Phi Alpha at U-Michigan and never threw without his Storm Gadget XF Wrist Support (southpaw)—a gunmetal plastic sheathing that stretched from the girth of his forearm to tip of his index. A wicked case of tendinitis in his late twenties (orthopedically scoped) had led him to find wrist support, and now, at thirty-seven, he couldn't roll without it. He never questioned if this was a physical or mental constraint.

As he rose from the orange plastic chair, his wife, Becca, pulled at the hem of his black tee. She mouthed *remember.* He nodded. He wasn't retarded. They'd spent the fifteen-minute drive discussing his expected etiquette—to be a *part of,* to understand that they were couples *having fun bowling,* not merely *bowling*—and he'd assured her that it was all good. He'd abide by her rules. But she'd kept going. Kept talking about his competitive streak. He'd gotten quiet then. The highway had been specks of red lights.

Jorge rolled a Brunswick Wicked Siege. He loved it. The ball was an optical illusion in color—either purple or black, depending upon overhead lighting—with a tasteful silver etching of Dr. Doom's metal facemask. He felt like it made a statement. Something aggressive. Something powerful. Something that merged the ball and him as one.

He lined his left foot four inches behind the dot on the thirty-board. He brought the ball to its birthplace, exactly three inches out from his clavicle and four inches from his left earlobe. This was the moment he loved. The quiet stillness of this five seconds. When it was he and the ball and the pins. The feel of Doom was just the right amount of heavy. The pinch of his fingers was just the right amount of pain. He felt the world drop away. His vision narrowed, tunneled. It settled on the thirty-board arrow. Every nerve ending in his body remembered the feeling of a perfect throw.

He was milliseconds away from starting his right foot forward—from starting the motion that had once been described as *breathtaking in its fluidity*—when he heard the voice of his wife telling Sandy and Daniel how *silly Jorge's bowling obsession was.*

His weight was already in motion. He couldn't stop thinking about this being a bitchy thing to say. Why would she say this during my approach? Does she have no respect for me?

For bowling? As he approached the foul line, he remembered his mother's same sentiment toward his father, how she couldn't understand how bowling was like religion to that man, the only thing that allowed him to function, to get through eight hours a day of scrubbing the shit of rich white men from the toilets of downtown skyscrapers, to return home with enough self-respect to demand Jorge look him in the eye. Jorge told himself to stop because his mind wasn't clear. He didn't. He kept going. He thought about Becca not even trying to understand what it all meant to him. Not caring in the slightest. The same with his mother. He let the ball go. The turnover of his wrist felt good. The wax job was on point and grabbed the ball, which increased in velocity with each rotation until it hooked directly into the pocket. The pins exploded into the backdrop.

Damn, that's good, he thought.

Jorge knew it was a rare night. He told himself not to think about it—the unobtainable three hundred—but he did. His stroke had felt that good.

⋮

Daniel Casoli sold bulk airfare to third-rate destinations like Gulfport and Laughlin and had performed cunnilingus on Becca six hours earlier in room 107 at the Lake Ilene Inn after the noon AA meeting and he'd told her it was love, what they were doing, how he felt, and she'd said something along the same lines, and that's when he'd suggested bowling, *let's do it, a double, just to be with you.*

So here he was, his arm around his wife, his eyes darting between Jorge, smug in his obvious skill on the lanes, and Becca, the blonde Ritz Carlton of his life. His wife, Sandy, took a slug of beer, finishing the plastic cup before the first frame. The smell of beer still gave him somewhat of a moist tongue. He'd asked her to maybe take it easy with the drinking tonight. This was in the parking lot on their way in, their arms intertwined. She'd said, "Yeah, I'll keep that in mind."

"See I have some work to do," he said to the group.

Jorge smiled. He had giant lower teeth, freakish really. Jorge said, "Just luck, brother, just luck."

"Go," Sandy said.

"I'm going, I'm going."

Daniel tried to make his last glance at Becca be meaningful, and it was, just like all the looks they shared—first across the decaying Uptown Alano Club from over the rims of white Styrofoam coffee cups, months later across forkfuls of strawberry and brie salad at the Lexington, her telling him about the *miracle of the mundane* and *letting go and letting God* and the *joy of living clean and sober*, and then just two months ago, the look they shared in room 107 for the first time, the guilt of breaking vows and taboos and the excitement and the secure knowledge that what they were doing was okay because their partners didn't understand what it was like to battle a foe more cunning and baffling than cancer—were better than anything, a secret, an understanding.

"Aim at the pins," Sandy said.

"The arrows, honey."

"For reals."

Daniel Casoli took his ball, an ungodly heavy black house ball, and brought it to his chin. Becca called out something about seeing those skills. This made him smile, his back to his wife, his grin visible to nobody except the ball. He aimed at the center arrow. He thought about the way Becca had crushed her nearly-perfect thighs around his head that afternoon, how this had created a seashore sound, waves crashing, waves receding.

He tossed his ball.

It knocked eight pins down, the two on the far right still standing.

He turned. Sandy poured another beer from the pitcher. She said, "Arrows, babe, arrows."

He gave her a placating smile. She gave him a mocking thumbs-up. He picked up his ball from the dispenser. Sometimes he wondered if he still loved Sandy. He held the ball inches from his mouth. He thought about her being selfish to continue to drink the way she did after everything that had happened, after how hard he'd worked at quitting—the DUI and outpatient and meetings and steps—and there she was, pounding Budweisers like it was the Armageddon, in front of Becca, nonetheless, even after the talk about her taking it easy tonight. He started his approach. Daniel wondered how to broach the subject with Becca. He didn't want to be the one who suggested they leave their partners. The ball hit the two pins. Daniel pumped his fist.

⋮

Becca Joyce-Rodriquez was the youngest of four sisters and couldn't fully bring herself to sing in the shower, settling for a continuous hum, telling herself it was just as good, and to her, bowling was Jorge's thing, always had been, always would be. She was beginning to think this whole evening had been a gross miscalculation on her part. Daniel's wife was getting salty; Jorge hadn't said but two words; Daniel, bless his heart, wouldn't stop staring.

"Bowling with some regular pros," she said.

"Maybe Jorge here," Daniel said. He slapped Jorge on the shoulder. Becca knew this was a mistake, Jorge hating to be touched. She went to squeeze her husband's hand but was greeted by his bionic arm. Then it was Sandy draining another glass and peering at Becca, saying things about wrist guards and arrows, and Daniel had been right: her drinking *was* bad. They'd been there, what, twenty minutes, and she was already openly mocking her husband.

No wonder he cheats.

"Seriously," Becca said. "You guys are some rock star bowlers."

"Then you're in good company," Daniel said. He seemed to be trying to keep his stare, which she wished he would stop doing. Jorge wasn't stupid. Neither was Sandy. Daniel just staring, staring, always, and she wanted to say *what?* What is so interesting? What are you trying to say? Use your words. Just stop looking.

"Go, baby," Jorge said.

Becca got up. She felt everyone's eyes on her—her husband's and Daniel's and Sandy's, but also the gazes of the group of teenagers the next lane over, the fifty-somethings two lanes from them—and that's how it'd always been. Becca the object of affection. Becca the baby of the family, her father's cheekbones, her mother's curves. She thought about her first dates with Jorge, him standing behind her, teaching her how to roll, how his warm breath was both repulsive and endearing. She lifted up her ball. It was lavender, a present from Jorge when he still tried to include her. She wanted to keep up with a strike. She heard Daniel bark bits of encouragement. She thought about how he'd finally said *I love you* earlier that afternoon. She'd had no idea how to react. She'd looked down between her legs. It was just Daniel's eyes peeking over the bald mound of her pelvis. She'd wanted to go back five minutes, to redirect the afternoon and their actions and then maybe two months before that and refuse to grab lunch and then months and months back, her choosing a different home group, her not confusing attention for esteem, and then she wanted to keep going back and to learn to control her drinking before it became daily and then she'd be a kid, her father's baby, putting her ear between the snaps of his flannel shirt, forgetting about sight, just listening to his breaths, his laughs, his little hairs tickling the cavern of her ear.

She bowled.

It made a beeline for the gutter.

"Shit."

"That's okay," Daniel said.

"Use the arrows, yo," Sandy said.

Jorge grinned, gave a wink.

Her next shot hit the middle of the pins. Seven of them toppled over, the eighth undecided, teetering, settling on staying upright.

⋮

"Here's to the shitty-ass game of bowling," Sandy said.

She raised her plastic cup, a Budweiser Lime logo on its side, her fifth. Nobody raised his or her own glasses. She said, "Figures." She smiled at Jorge because he understood being confined in a prison of holier-than-thou marital sobriety. Daniel placed his hand on her back, but it was more controlling than loving.

"So I'm just going to go ahead and throw it out there," Sandy said. "Bro, what's up with the wrist thing?"

Jorge cited something about an injury.

"Because I'm like Transformer Arm is straight up killing it, you know? Maybe need one of those things myself."

"You're up, honey," Daniel said.

"No shit."

"Well?"

The pressure of his backrub increased.

"Silly me," Sandy said. "Thought we were here to socialize. I mean, that's what it's about, right, bowling? Talking. Am I wrong?"

"Absolutely," Becca said. "That's what I've been telling Jorge here."

Sandy watched her lean over and kiss her husband's check. She wondered how her own skin would look against his, the contrast, if she'd look paler or darker.

"My girl knows what's up".

"Are you going to go?" Daniel asked.

"Are you going to dig your fingernail through my spine?"

Sandy watched her husband play that one off like it was a joke, the two of them in on it, the two of them such tricksters, always giving one another hard times. But that's how it used to be, Sandy thought. They were fun fun, the life of any party. She thought about the first time they'd met, a party their senior year at UC, an ugly sweater party, Daniel wearing some inside-out woven number, just hideous, them meeting eyes through a crowd of people who suddenly didn't matter, them doing shots, their laughs louder than everyone's, sex on a basement couch, the quietest moment after climax, his face little-boy sincere with his hooded eyes, him saying *I think I'm in love.*

Daniel let out a nice laugh, loud and fake. But she could tell she'd pushed him far enough because the edges of his nostril flared and this had been happening more and more since his sobriety, what with his over-sensitivity. He was no longer able to take her barbing. He was...just fucking say it: my husband is *different.*

She finished the flat backwash in her cup. She reached for the pitcher. It was empty. She said, "Damn Jorge, slow your roll."

"Was all you, hon," Becca said.

Sandy wouldn't stoop to Becca's level of I'm-a-better-person-than-you-because-I'm-sober, so she said the next thing that crossed her mind: "Shit ain't going to fill itself."

Becca looked down into her lap. Daniel's hand slid off Sandy's back. Jorge just sat there boring as fuck. And then she felt stupid because she'd done something wrong, that much was obvious. She just didn't know what. This was happening more and more. She stood, laughing, saying, "Jesus, it's not like I fiddled a little boy." She grabbed the pitcher and headed toward the bar.

⋮

Jorge lied to his wife, telling her he'd had two glasses, although he really was still on his first. She kept saying are you sure, are you sure? He nodded. He didn't want to talk. He didn't want to wait for drunk Sandy to come back and continue her attempts at ruining his perfect game—*Don't put the P-label on it*—because he knew a confrontation between anyone would be detrimental to what he had going.

"Baby, I could have sworn you only had one glass," Becca said.

Jorge glanced at Daniel, who quickly averted his gaze. Jorge felt bad for him. Sandy was acting like an idiot. And now, he had to sit there pretending like he wasn't hearing Becca slander his wife.

"Jorge, please, go ahead and bowl. It's no big deal," Daniel said.

"Not a problem."

"I'm sorry, she's not normally like this."

"Do you want me to talk to her?" Becca asked.

"No. I don't know. No, not tonight."

"She's fine," Jorge said.

"Maybe I should go...you know." Daniel stood. Becca nodded. Jorge just wanted them to figure it out, to get back down there, to continue with the game.

Once Daniel was out of earshot, Becca turned to Jorge. Her face was a pinched *what the fuck.* She said, "Can you be anymore of a jerk?"

"What?"

"We talked about this. I mean, God, you've said all of ten words."

"You're kidding me?"

"I wish."

Jorge shook his head. He couldn't believe he somehow had ended up as the bad guy. He couldn't be distracted; that's what this fight would be. He envisioned his roll. The flawless gliding of foot and knee and arm and wrist, just the right amount of rollover, the pins exploding.

"You always do this," Becca said.

Jorge adjusted the gauge on his wrist protector.

"Just tune out. Pretend you aren't even here. I mean, for once, that's all I asked, *just this once* to be sociable."

Jorge couldn't take the chance of responding because coiled on the tip of his tongue were insults he'd shelved for years. How could she be so clueless? So selfish to not understand the stakes of what he had going? It'd been the one thing he'd strived for his entire life. He thought of his father sitting at the head of the table, his dark skin a stark contrast with the yellow wallpaper. Jorge heard his mother yelling about mold in the drain and needing a water heater that actually worked. He saw his father's face still and unflinching, his bare chest showing through the black league-issued bowling shirt, the wide white collars always pressed and steamed. It was no surprise he'd left; a man can only take so much. Jorge looked at the electronic scoreboard. Strike after strike after strike. His father had never done it, perfection. He got up and started walking away.

Becca said, "That's nice. Walk away. That's good."

Jorge climbed the three carpeted steps. He looked behind the register. A guy he only knew by mustache shook his head as if to say *I see what you have going here.* Beyond the register, he could make out Sandy at the bar, Daniel at her side, his hands pleading. He thought about all the games he'd rolled in his life—thousands, each one in the pursuit of a single goal—and he thought about two-fifty-nine being his PB. He thought about Becca making this sliver of a chance about her. *You're not doing this, you're not doing that.* And walking into the men's room, he let himself think for the first time that life was better when his wife was still a drunk because at least he could give her selfishness an excuse.

⋮

The bathroom door swung into the wall when Daniel Casoli walked in. He saw Jorge pissing at the far end of the trough and this made him annoyed, wanting a brief moment to regroup, splash some water on his face, pop an Altoid.

"Some game you've got going out there," Daniel said.

"Oh. Thanks."

Daniel walked to the far side of the four-foot basin. He took out his penis. He said, "I mean, you could be looking at a perf—"

"Ahh!"

This sudden yell halted Daniel's stream. *What the hell?* He realized it was probably like baseball, how nobody mentioned a potential no-hitter while it was in progress.

"Sorry," Daniel said.

"It's fine."

They pissed. Clumps of chew littered the metal trough. Daniel couldn't help but get the feeling that Jorge's piss was coming towards him, which it was, the angle designed that way, but its gushing felt somehow violent.

"About everything," Daniel said. "I don't know what's going on with Sandy. She normally isn't like this...and, I don't know...sorry, I guess."

Daniel wished his mouth would stop moving. That he would quit with the blanket apologies. He wondered if he really was apologizing for *it*—the fact he'd just been with Jorge's wife that very afternoon, that it had been going on for two months, that declarations of love had been exchanged, that it was only a matter of time until he would take Becca as his lover, rightfully-so, legally, in front of the eyes of God, forever. But guilt wasn't part of it, not when what he and Becca had was so *right.* Sure, feelings would be hurt, both Jorge's and Sandy's, but it was different, what they had, their love like that of movies.

The piss streaming down the trough was a late-season harvest gold. Daniel didn't realize he was doing it, following the liquid to its riverhead, but he was, and there *it* was, the biggest penis he'd ever seen in person. Holy shit. And just as involuntarily, he glanced at his own modest German-sized member, and his mind was the drain in the trough and it was jealousy at the vision of Becca loving that *thing* over there and it housing itself inside of where he'd been in room 107 and then it was the thought of never really satisfying Becca, that he'd understood this at a base level, that's why he'd spent so much time downstairs with his mouth. He pictured husband and wife doing husband and wife things. He could practically feel the thundering post-urination shakes of Jorge as he finished up an arm's length away. He *was* perfect—his perfect penis and perfect game—and Daniel couldn't help the thoughts that came—*you will never be good enough, everybody else has some unnamable thing figured out, an inside joke, that's it, and you are the fucking punch line*—and his lips moved, the serenity prayer his only learned defense. Daniel quickly told himself that it was different, what he and Becca had. They shared the same feelings, the need to numb oneself in the whirlpool of drink, to escape, to be somebody else, to feel appreciated for hour-long lunch dates, to simply connect.

Jorge said he'd see him back out there. Daniel finished the last bit of his delicate trickle. He mouthed *and the wisdom to know the difference*. He knew he had to be the one to put his cards on the table—*Becca, I want to be with you, for real*—and it had to be tonight.

⋮

Becca sat there on the rigid orange chair. The alley had filled up, every lane taken, people waiting for their turn. People cheered and hollered. She studied the teenagers to her left with their sagged skinny jeans and sweeping bangs. She remembered that time. How things were all in the future tense. And then Becca looked at the fifties on the other side. They were more subdued, rhythmic in their head nods and high-fives, but they seemed happy in routine, in each other. Becca thought about being thirty-four, how it wasn't young and it wasn't old, a phony age, one when they were supposed to have their shit together career-wise, family-wise, kids, budding 401K's, weeklong trips over the summer to the mountains, camping, cheap and fun and the sun rising over fourteen-thousand-foot peaks, their own memories. Nobody seemed to be looking at her. And then she thought about a saying in AA—*feeling alone in a crowd of a thousand*—and she'd fought with this mindset her entire life, and it was more AA clichés—*to be uniquely alone, trudging the road to happy destiny*—and she wondered if everyone felt these things, not just those who'd ruined their lives with alcohol. Maybe bowling was invented so people could escape from this crushing weight for ten dollars and a few hours. Leagues and routine and being a regular or an activity or double date or an outing, all of it a distraction as good as an affair or glass of red.

"Leave for five minutes and my girl looks like she's 'bout to slit her wrists," Sandy said. She stood at the end of the four-person table, fresh pitcher in hand.

Becca felt something close to relief at another person.

"Where the boys?" Sandy asked.

"Restroom."

"Playing swords?"

"Sorry?"

Sandy laughed. She sat down and poured herself what had to be her sixth drink. Becca watched how Sandy's eyes closed when the cup touched her lips. She imagined the tickle of bubbles brushing against her own nose. She knew what Sandy felt. She did. That it was the only way, a reward for working, for living, for socializing, for making it this long on the earth.

"There's a different way," Becca said.

"What's up?"

"A different way, than…" She pointed at the cup.

Sandy smirked. She trained her eyes directly into Becca's. She said, "Knew *this* was coming."

"I'm not here to lecture or—"

"No, no. Go ahead. Let's hear it. Really. I mean, that's why we're sitting here, right? The whole bowling thing. The boys *disappearing*. For this moment, the one where you tell me about Twelve Steps and powerlessness. How great life is. How am I doing so far?"

"You think you have it all figured out, don't you?"

Sandy shook her head. She said, "Nope, not at all. But I'm not sitting here fronting like I do."

Becca fought the urge to tell Sandy that she'd made her husband come that very day, that he'd professed his love for her, not Sandy, that maybe this was due to Sandy's drinking, her disregard for what Daniel was going through. Instead, she said, "Funny, because that's what you seem to be doing. Telling me what I'm going to do, just like *you* have it all figured out."

Sandy leaned back, stretching, pushing her breasts out, and then rested both elbows on the table dividing them.

"Listen, you seem like a nice enough woman. Really, you do. But I'll be motherfucked if I let you sit here passing judgments about being better than me."

"That's not what I'm saying."

"Then what is it?"

"I'm trying to tell you that you don't need to drink like you do. That's it. That's all I have to say."

"So I can be like...you? Stop drinking, pray to God, go on pretending life is some magical fucking quest?"

"Never mind."

"Or is it so I can have your life? That's what you all say, right? *Want what she has?* So you want me to see you with your trashy push-up bra with the lace showing, your hundred-dollar haircut, your *ethnic* husband who doesn't talk, and frankly, seems to like bowling a whole lot more than you, and all of this is supposed to make me see the errors in my ways, make me jealous?"

Nobody had ever talked to Becca like this before. She had no idea how to respond. She caught herself dabbing the corner of her right eye. She would not be reduced to tears. Sandy wasn't worth it. She wasn't worth anything. Certainly not

Daniel's affection or faithfulness. Becca felt like everyone in the entire alley was staring, was waiting for her to finally let go, to snap, to become something other than what she was. She spoke from unmoving lips: "I feel sorry for you."

Sandy reached across the table. She patted Becca's hand. She said, "No, honey, least I know I'm a mess. You, babe, haven't the slightest fucking clue."

.
.
.

Sandy looked at the overhead scoreboard and was like thank God this night is almost over with. She laughed at her scores, each turn basically a little worse than the previous. She didn't really care that her ball was a shitty shade of pink.

She lined up like she'd seen Jorge do, his feet just behind the dots. She realized Daniel had quit with the advice and encouragement and this made her pause. She lost a step of balance and regained it, the ball almost dropping, her almost dropping. She turned around and said, "Walking's new to this bitch." She was met by three smiles, each one the same, each one lifeless, pencil drawings on plastic mannequins. This was the image she started forward with. People becoming distant. People not really people. People there to humor her, to tell her *good job, maybe next time, you have such potential, that's okay.*

Her ball traveled the length of the lane in the gutter.

Eighteen months before, Daniel would have been doubled over with laughter, the only sound that little catch he made when he couldn't get enough air.

She turned. Daniel didn't say anything, barely made eyes. Jorge studied his stupid wrist thing. That bitch Becca stared off at the middle-aged grouping to their right. Sandy walked off the actual lanes. She wedged her way between her husband's knees. She said, "Any pointers, Daddy?"

He shook his head.

"Come on, what am I doing wrong?"

Again it was the shaking of his head. This felt like a betrayal because that's who Daniel had become, the supportive husband, the caretaker, the advice giver, and he wouldn't engage, wouldn't even tell her about the arrows, so that's what she said, running the back of her fingernails down his check, "What was that thing about the arrows?"

He turned his face away from her touch. He said, "Please just finish."

Sandy gave a snort. She said, "Fun night." She took her ball and she held it and she wanted her husband to tell her what she needed to do to succeed. She studied the largest arrow in the middle of the lane. She'd bowl it straight. She'd bowl it down the middle and knock the pins over. *Was it all her fault?* And then it was the thoughts that she'd pushed him too far, like all he asked was for her to keep it under control, that this night meant a lot to him, and she aimed with every morsel of concentration and took three steps and let the ball go.

It started straight; it ended up in the gutter.

Sandy thought this was the best she could do and maybe it wasn't good enough. She didn't want to face Daniel because he'd moved on from trying and his mouth would be that tight-lipped smile or even worse, nothing at all, so she stayed facing the lanes and felt the reverberation of bowled balls from the wood through her shoes and then she felt the music too.

⋮

Jorge's first roll of the tenth frame was perfect—*go ahead and say it, perfect*—the pins not having a chance at staying upright. He was two rolls away from The Unobtainable. Two rolls away from dropping the *un*, from becoming one of nine other people he knew of in Denver to reach the fabled three hundred. To reach perfection.

"Come on, baby, you can do it," Becca said.

He wouldn't turn around. Didn't want to mess with his concentration.

She'd changed her tune, no longer Angry Wife with her you-need-to-be-different comments because she must have finally understood what was happening, what he was about to accomplish. A lifetime achievement. He told himself he loved her for understanding or at least pretending to.

Four inches behind the dot on the thirty-board.

Envision the approach, the release, the follow-through, everything smooth, molasses sliding down a mason jar.

Doom settled into the lane with a love-tap spanking and hugged the gutter and then curved and kept curving and it was going to be perfect, just south of the backside of the One. The pins tumbled.

People cheered. The lanes to either side had quit and now watched. The workers stood behind him. People raised their fists. A few clapped. A catcall sounded from a few lanes over. Becca held her hands in front of her face as if praying. It was Jorge talking to himself, trying to block out the building tension, the buzz of hushed voices, of excitement at witnessing the amazing: *concentrate, this is you, you can do this, one more roll.* He picked up his ball. He rubbed down the metal mask etched into its purple-black surface. He spoke to it, the ball, his persona, the silent title he'd dubbed himself, Doom. We can do this. Just give me this. God, please, just give me this.

He lined up.

He ratcheted one more degree of guidance from his Storm Gadget XF Wrist Support.

And then it was quiet. The gathered crowd ceased to exist. His wife's calls and Daniel's stares and Sandy's drunken slurs were all gone, his life boiled down to him versus ten wooden pins. Doom radiated pure love and destruction and empathy. He channeled every game played and every ball rolled and every pin struck. He started forward. His release felt spot-on. Life in slow motion. Everything crumbled away to him alone with Doom. The two of them could conquer anything. The two of them were lovers and friends and that's all he needed and ever would. He watched his best friend travel sixty feet. Then it happened: the pins fell, each and every one of them.

Jorge dropped to his knees. His eyes filled. He heard screaming and cheering but it was just noise. He dreaded the back slaps and hugs he knew were coming. He never wanted to move. To be anywhere else. For it all to end. He watched the mechanical arm come down, clear his pins into the backdrop. He wondered if his father would have been any happier achieving this, if he would have stayed. Ten fresh pins were put in their place. It was over that fast, everything he'd ever wanted, perfection.

⋮

Their game was interrupted with strangers congratulating Jorge. Daniel watched as the owner came out, a hairy man, not altogether unlike a pin himself, and shook Jorge's hand, presenting him with a small plaque engraved with *300* on its golden surface.

Becca sat back down after kissing her husband. Daniel thought about Jorge's giant penis between those lips, the same set he'd kissed earlier that afternoon. This was too much, this thought, Becca with anyone else, sexually or physically or emotionally, and she'd said it that day: *I love you, too.*

All that was left of Sandy was a plastic cup. She'd gone off to return her shoes. Daniel thought her missing out on everything was fitting. Just like it'd been over the last eighteen months with her drinking, her not growing, not changing, and Daniel experiencing life for the first time without the inebriation of alcohol, without being numb, and that was it, he thought, simple as that: I've grown into a different person.

He made eyes at Becca. She smiled, her lipstick still evenly applied. It was now or never; they couldn't go on living this double-life.

He leaned across the table. Becca glanced over at Jorge, still being congratulated. Daniel said, "We need to talk."

"What?"

"Talk. Us. About us."

"Not now," Becca said. She glanced back at her husband.

"I can't do this anymore, the lying. I need to…to be—"

"Stop, okay?"

"I need to be with you."

Becca laughed. It was beautiful and hurtful and he had no idea what was funny and he took her hand and she tried to pull away but he held her firm, his fingers cinched around her tiny wrist.

"We can't keep doing this. It's not fair, to them. We need to let—"

Becca yanked her hand free. She said, "You need to stop."

Becca's coldness wasn't making sense. He tried to meet her gaze, to communicate through silent understanding. Her attention darted between Jorge and Daniel and her cuticles. "Baby," Daniel said. She shook her head. He thought about her doing the same thing against the pillow earlier that afternoon. He said, "You, I choose *you.*" Her head kept shaking. This wasn't supposed to be happening. He'd worked so hard in his new life and it was all for her, he understood that, the DUI, the meetings, Sandy's drinking, all of it to get him into that Tuesday noon meeting months before, to get him to the woman who returned his stare, who spoke of love without having to open her mouth.

"I'm not going to leave," Becca said.

"What?"

"Jorge. I won't."

"Becca, what we have—"

"Is nothing. A fantasy. An excuse."

With that, she stood, walking over to Jorge, wrapping her arms around him, standing on her tiptoes, kissing his chin. This wasn't right, not even a little bit. He replayed the conversation, his words, hers, and she'd said love, she'd fucking said it not seven hours before. He felt a hand on his shoulder. For the briefest of moments, he let himself believe it was Becca's, her French manicured-fingers rubbing his back, telling him it was okay, they'd figure it out, that she was sorry she'd hurt his feelings.

"The fuck's going on?" Sandy said.

Daniel shrugged. He leaned his head into his wife's soft stomach. She petted his hair. He closed his eyes and tried to convince himself it was Becca behind him, and when that failed, that Sandy's embrace was still good enough.

⋮

There Becca stood under her husband's arm, the entire alley still watching, still coming up for a fist bump or hand shake. And she smiled. She smiled and smiled and smiled because maybe life and marriage were this easy, to stand by the side of her partner soaking in the leftover stares. She glanced at Daniel. Sandy rubbed his hair. He'd get over it. She thought about what it'd meant and maybe it was as simple as wanting to know she still had it or maybe it was that Jorge didn't pay her enough attention or maybe it was because Daniel had made her feel special. That's it. Special. That's all she'd ever wanted. To matter. She rested her head in the nook of her husband's chest and it was her father in those quiet childhood moments and she looked at their resting balls—black and purple-black and off-pink and lavender—all siting in a straight line, their slicked sides touching.

She spoke into Jorge's black T-shirt: "You love me?"

He didn't say anything. He stared at the electronic monitor hanging from the ceiling. Red block letters flashed *!PERFECT!* He probably hadn't heard. She pressed her ear harder to his chest. She said, "I'm sorry." People stared. *!PERFECT!* Jorge said something and it was either *I did it* or *I get it* and he walked away to the ball retriever. He took his ball, rubbing it with a cloth he kept in his back pocket. Then it was the sound of balls rolling, of pins exploding, of people laughing and joking as Split This! reanimated itself, kept going, people squeezing out the last few hours of game and companionship before returning home in cold cars to dark homes alone or together.

Tiny Dancer

It was a Thursday, and I danced in the shower. This was after gym class. Philip Stoltz played his stereo. You can't really blame me. I mean, that song, the *check it out now, I'm a funk soul brother*, it's catchy. It has a good rhythm. I danced. In a roomful of twenty naked fourteen-year-olds.

It was slight at first. Just some bobbing of my head. I think my knees were next. Maybe it was some shuffling. The water over my eyes, my hips might have joined in. My shoulders. I try not to think about it. I know at one point my ass was really moving. Philip told Isabella that it was like a backup girl in a rap video.

They all laughed. I opened my eyes (guess they had been closed). Philip Stoltz suggested that I was a faggot. Everyone ran from the showers. The soap stung.

By lunch, it was settled upon: *Tiny Dancer*. Philip told this to my face. He probably thought he was better than me because he'd gotten his braces off that summer.

"Get it?" he said.

I got it.

"Because your dick's tiny."

Yup.

"Tiny Dancer. Like the song."

I offered up maybe he was gay for knowing an Elton John song.

He socked me in the stomach.

By Chemistry, everyone knew. Girls looked at me, which normally didn't happen. I thought Isabella Lopez checked out my dills, as if to corroborate the story she'd been told.

Isabella sat in front of me. Her hair reminded me of a broom. I'd told her this the first day of school. Her eyes had become the smallest of slits. I'd told her a good broom. One made of silk. But dry. Kind of like hay. I liked it when she wore tight tops because I could see her bra strap. I thought about pulling it back and letting it snap. I thought she would like this, like how my mom would giggle when my dad slapped her heinie after dinner. I liked it best when Isabella Lopez wore dark colored bras under her shirts. Thursday was one of those days. A perfect storm of a yellow top, black bra. Sometimes I thought about lying with my head on her back and slipping her bra around my throat. I'm not sure why, but this always seemed so sexy.

⋮

I, of course, walked home that day. I normally got a ride from my sister, Shelly, who was older and pretty and rather slutty. She hated giving me rides. I had to walk across the parking lot and down two blocks because she couldn't run the risk of being seen with me in her car. Sometimes she would drive by and wave.

That Thursday, I didn't even wait down the block. I walked to Hidden Falls overlooking the South Platte. I threw rocks. I couldn't hear them hit the water. I recognized kids from school, the older ones. They did drugs. One of them called out, "Might as well just jump."

⋮

That night, we sat around plates of quinoa and two ounces of salmon per. Both my parents were all about *brain food.* We said grace, praying to no god in particular, just the *idea of love*, as my father called it. I ate my plateful in seconds. Shelly said, "Pass the soy milk, *Tiny Dancer.*"

I prayed my dad hadn't heard.

Shelly laughed. She had dimples and blond hair and was a senior and went to parties two nights a week. I knew she was getting pounded by TJ Prunty. I read that very fact scratched into the locker room stall. There was a drawing, too. I took a picture for proof.

"Tiny Dancer?" my dad said.

"Yup," Shelly said.

"Like the song?"

"Yeah, that's what everyone's calling him."

He put his hand on mine. This was to get me to meet his eyes. I didn't look over.

He sang, *Hold me close....*

Everyone laughed

"Just messing with you." With his fingers still on my hand, he asked what happened.

"Nothing."

"Fred's got a little dick. And he's gay. He tried to slow dance with the other freshmen in the shower."

I would show them the cartoon depiction of slutty Shelly. I wondered who the other penis was. If that, in fact, was an accurate addition to the drawing.

"What is this?" my father asked. I glanced over. He was nothing but beard and glasses, a disgusting rat-tail of a ponytail resting limply on his left shoulder. "Fred, you know whatever you choose to do, whatever *sex* you are attracted to…"

"I like girls."

My mom held my other arm. "Oh, sweetie, you can love whoever you want."

My dad said, "But I do find it a little hard to believe, the part about you having a small…"

"If he's anything like you," my mom said.

"Jesus fuck," Shelly yelled.

I wanted to die.

"I'm just saying," my mom said.

"I'm going to vomit," Shelly said.

"Do you want me to take a look at it?" my dad asked.

"What? No."

"Just offering." My dad let go of my arm, leaning back in his chair. "Nothing to be embarrassed about."

"You wonder why I never have friends over," Shelly said.

"We're all family. If you ask me, that's half the problem with the world today. Everyone afraid of his or her own sexuality."

I might have heard his zipper.

"Your father's right," my mom added.

I prayed for death, not necessarily having to be quick or painless.

⋮

Later that night, I stole my mom's measuring tape from her sewing box. The Internet said the average penile size was between 5.5' to 6.5' inches. I thought of Isabella Lopez. Not wanting to shortchange myself, I surfed around until I found the perfect photograph. It was on the Marshall's website. A picture of a skinny Hispanic girl with a shadow of a mustache in a cotton tee, a dark bra underneath.

And when I really pushed the ruler into my stomach, I was on the higher side of the average. Maybe I would tell this to Philip Stoltz.

⋮

My next morning went like this:
>*Tiny Dancer*—nod.
>*Tiny Dancer*—smile.
>*Tiny Dancer*—look over my shoulder like it wasn't me.
>*Tiny Dancer*—God, make it stop.

And then there was gym with the boring volleyball unit. I dreaded the mandatory post-PE shower. Mr. Frankie waited in his little office that used to be the sporting goods closet. He'd sit there, and we had to go in one by one. Newspaper clips of TJ Prunty hung on the wall. It always smelled like Fire Hot Cheetos. Mr. Frankie would smell our hair, then our armpits.

Sometimes I thought he smelled my neck, too. I never understood how this constituted as not being molesty as fuck, but he was big and tough and the girls wanted to sleep with him and the boys wanted to be him.

I undressed in the stall. I knew I was 5.76 inches when erect. This was above average. I shook it around a little to make it actually hang instead of stick straight out like a gumdrop. I walked toward the showers. It was too quiet. I put my clothes on the blue wooden bench. I peered inside the cave of nudity and athlete's foot. My classmates stood underneath the faucets. They didn't laugh or joke or call me names. *Maybe it passed?* The only head still open was in the back. I made myself skinny as to not touch any naked flesh. I stood under the freezing water. All the fluffing I did in the stall was for naught; my cock looked like a cat's nose.

Then I heard it. Philip Stoltz's little boombox. It was *Tiny Dancer.* The water was suddenly hot. My skin felt like it was going to peel off. I pretended not to notice, but everyone stared and pointed, and the laughing grew to a crescendo. I wanted to be anyone else. Philip started throwing towels to everyone. They soaked them. The first snap across my kidney stung worse than when I was five years old and closed the backdoor with my foot still in the way. A slap against my face. Then it was constant and I curled into a ball and they chanted *Tiny Dancer* and hollered and it was excruciating, the humiliation. They cheered when an extra loud slapping of flesh echoed throughout the dungeon that was the group shower.

I covered my cock and face.

My lip bled onto the pissed-on floor.

When I finally got dressed, I walked into chemistry late. Ms. Putter stopped me when I came in. She pulled me outside and she held onto my arm, which made me feel good and bad all at once. "Who did this to you?"

I didn't say anything.

"Fred, talk to me. Who did this?"

I thought about telling. Getting every single cocksucker in the ninth grade third period PE class expelled or at least suspended. I played the tape forward, the threats and everyone hating me even more, them calling me *Snitch Faggot Tiny Dancer.*

"I fell."

"Fred, please, this can't go on."

"I know."

"Do you want to go see the nurse?"

"No."

I walked back inside and took my seat behind Isabella Lopez. Ms. Putter came in. She was visually upset, her cheeks flushed. She had trouble remembering where we'd left off the day before. As she talked, I traced the edge of Andra's bra through her shirt with my eyes. I could almost feel the slight rise of the fabric, the millimeter difference between her tea-colored skin and B cup.

Don't ask me why, but I did it. As hard as I could. No thought. I pulled back her strap like a bow and arrow. I let go. The sound of elastic slapping skin. She screamed. She turned. I waved.

I was sent to the dean's office.

⋮

I told a beautiful story about there being a bug on Andra's back. I made up a Latin name for the species, which made Dean Rudolph cringe. I told her I was trying to brush it off because these specific bugs can be dangerous, like they burrowed into your skin and lay eggs, and I was merely trying to help. I told her the bug had already started its digging, that's the reason I must have pulled her...but I was just helping.

Dean Rudolph was a woman with short Ringo Starr hair who blinked a lot. I wondered if she had a condition. She agreed that what I did was not bad.

"Good even?" I asked.

"Sure."

Blink-blink. Blink-blink.

"What happened to your face?"

"I got a little carried away popping zits."

"There's medication for that."

"Yeah."

"Do you want me to phone your mother about it?"

"Sorry?"

"There's Retin A, Accutane."

"No, that's quite all right."

Blinky-Blinkerton. It was beyond distracting.

"Are you excited about the dance?" she asked.

I wondered what her favorite Beatles' song was. Probably one Ringo sang, maybe *Yellow Submarine.*

I shrugged.

"You're going, aren't you, Fred?"

I couldn't think of anything worse. "Doubt it."

"What? You have to go. It will be a great time. The freshman school council has worked so hard. The theme is, oh, what do you call those parties now days?" I shook my head. She blinked. "Oh, you know the ones on television. The lights and glow sticks."

"Raves."

"Yes, *raves.* We even rented a smoke machine."

"Wow."

"Wow is right. You simply have to come. It's important to partake in such activities."

I wanted to ask if her condition was contagious.

"So can I plan on seeing you tonight?"

I nodded.

"Promise?"

"Fine."

$$\vdots$$

It was seventh period when Dean Rudolph hugged me goodbye, which, like Ms. Putter's touches, made me feel weird inside. I walked down the hall. Isabella Lopez talked to a group of cool kids. They all turned, followed me, daggers not even deadly enough for what was shooting from their eyes.

Tiny Dancer—guilty as charged.

Tiny Dancer—who, me?

Tiny Dancer—this isn't my life.

Tiny   Dancer—5.76   inches.

I knew it probably wasn't a good time to inquire if Isabella was going to the dance.

"Are you going to the dance?" I asked.

"Are you fucking retarded?"

"I'll take that as a *yes?*"

"You're such a freak," Isabella said.

"And your sister's a whore," Philip added for good measure.

At least they didn't know about my dad.

"And your dad looks like David Koresh," he said.

I left early that day, just walked out.

⋮

I sat on the sandstone bluff at Hidden Falls. I kicked the heels of my shoes against the rock. Some of it crumbled. The water was down there somewhere. I thought about jumping. I wondered if it would hurt. I figured it would, me breaking bones along the branches of the trees shielding the water. I'd probably just break my neck. I'd be cruising the halls in a mouth-operated two-wheeler. I wondered if Dean Rudolph wanted to sit on my face. Tiny Dancer was better than faggot. I cursed myself for snapping Isabella's bra. I threw a rock. It made no sound.

I wasn't going to jump, so I climbed up the bluff, and headed back to the small parking lot. My sister's car was there, but I didn't see her in the front seat. I walked closer. She was straddling TJ Prunty in the back, nothing but pasty flesh wiggling about. She looked over and screamed.

I turned and started walking away. A few seconds later TJ came rushing out of the car. It was like his brain could barely form the words, like they were suffocated in stupidity and overly-developed muscles.

"You sick fag," he gurgled. "What kind of sick fag watches his sister like that? I'm talking to you, you sick fag."

I understood he believed me to be a *sick fag*, perhaps his repetition was unneeded.

He was huge and Norwegian. I came up to his pecs. He held onto my arms. I looked at his face, waiting.

"Stop," Shelly yelled. She was at his side.

I wanted the massive steak of flesh to come down over my face.

"Fucking stop," she said again.

"But he's a sick fag," TJ said.

"Just cool it."

TJ couldn't seem to comprehend the situation.

"Go back to the car," she said.

Shelly zipped up her pants. I tried not to watch but I did. What the fuck was wrong with me?

"You're not going to tell, are you, Freddy?"

I shook my head.

"Cuz we weren't even doing anything."

"Yeah."

"Kissing is all."

"Okay."

"What happened to your face?" Shelly asked.

"I fell."

"You get beat-up?"

I nodded.

"You okay?"

"I'm okay."

"You need a ride?"

"No."

"You sure?"

"I'm sure."

⋮

My confirmation suit didn't really fit anymore, but it was tan, which I thought was cool. I decided not to wear socks, like the two-inch gap between the hem and my ankle was on purpose. I combed my hair straight back. I took a deep breath. I was in the parking lot. Parents dropped off their kids. My peers wore jeans and T-shirts and some of the girls had tube tops with their tits spilling out. Nobody looked as fly as I did.

Dean Rudolph and Ms. Putter sold tickets. They fawned over me. They told me how glad they were to see me, that I looked so sharp. I couldn't tell if Dean Rudolph was winking or blinking. I pulled out my five dollars and Dean Rudolph told me my money was no good there (definitely a wink).

I decided to get a lay of the land first. I walked around the darkened gymnasium. I thought the disco ball and strobe light were nice touches. The smoke machine was the size of a lunchbox. It dribbled steam in a two-foot radius.

I didn't respond to a single *Tiny Dancer* or *loser* or *faggot*. I concentrated, got in the zone. I saw Isabella. She stood along the wall with a pack of her friends. She wore the thinnest of white tops, jeans that hugged her body like dripped wax. It's like she knew. Like she did it on purpose. I could see it from across the basketball court: the darkest bra that had ever cradled those mounds of desire.

I walked up to the DJ. He wore baggy clothes and a backward hat.

"What's good, bro?"

"Pretty much nothing at all."

"What you want to hear?"

I told him my two requests.

I waited. I took off my jacket, careful to not wrinkle it against the back of a chair. I did some light stretching. I undid the button strangling me and lowered my tie an inch or two. I missed the pressure around my neck so I tightened it back up.

My song came on. The root of the latest chapter in the tragedy that was my life. Everyone turned just in time to see me burst onto the dance floor.

I crouched real low, letting the music pick up steam. It built and built. The circle of classmates closed in and they probably pointed and laughed like they always did, but I just looked at my loafers and bare ankles.

The breakdown came over the speakers and I exploded into a star, my arms outstretched.

Right about now, I'm a funk soul brother.

I curled into a tight ball and did it again. Four times in a row. I closed my eyes as tight as I could because I couldn't endure their looks. I felt the bass somewhere deep inside. My hands swayed above my head, picking up some sort of centrifugal force, causing my head to gyrate in the opposite direction. I was bent over, my moneymaker sashaying in roundabout arcs.

I was pretty sure I heard cheering

I slapped my ass. It stung. I did it again.

Check it out now, I'm a funk soul brother.

There was some robot.

My eyes closed, I was the music.

My eyes closed, I was invisible. I imagined Mr. Frankie in his windbreaker leaning against the wall, nodding his head in approval. Dean Rudolph would be front and center, clapping and blinking, humming *Yellow Submarine*. Ms. Putter was probably snapping her fingers as best she could. I danced like energy or light or God and there wasn't a molecule of air I couldn't move through, couldn't dislodge, couldn't incorporate into my life. With my eyes closed, I could see Philip Stoltz and all the other boys, and they would be speechless because I was better than them, not only because I could laugh at myself, but because I would be crushing girls, Isabella Lopez laying down, beckoning me over, begging me to put my back to hers, gently slipping underneath her bra strap like a down comforter on so many winter nights.

The music stopped. It was like I expected. Hundreds of open mouths, fingers pointing. My next song came on. Yes, it was *Tiny Dancer*. Isabella's friends pushed her. She fought back, but they kept pushing. She relented. She walked over.

She was the most beautiful thing I had ever seen, like live birth and maple sap dripping from a freshly tapped tree.

I knew it wasn't real, but I wanted to pretend. To believe she saw me for whom I was: a boy who was misunderstood and sexy, who had backne but would outgrow it, for somebody who had given up and joined in on his own cannibalization.

She laughed and couldn't meet my eyes and people chanted *dance, dance.*

I wanted to tell her you will get a marketing degree from the University of Northern Colorado. That this will translate into a glorified secretary job. That you will have kids with an unfaithful husband. That your left leg will become the deepest of purples from varicose veins. That you missed out. That I've loved you since I saw you in the hallway in seventh grade. That I would have treated you right.

But I didn't. I extended my hands. She extended hers. They rested on my shoulders, mine on her hips. I could feel her bones. They made me think of museums. I told myself not to look at her black bra, but fucking Christ, the lace above the cups was showing. And I told myself that it was real—everything—Isabella wanting to dance with me and everyone's jokes were jealousies and Dean Rudolph and Ms. Putter knew I would do great things and my dick simply hadn't been given the jolt of puberty and Shelly's compassion at Hidden Falls wasn't merely her emotional bribery and my father was normal, not losing his fucking mind, normal, and they loved me, everyone.

Elton John begged to be held closer. Smoke from the machine
sputtered across the gym floor. We were the only two dancing,
the only two.

The Woman with Size Thirteen Jimmy Choos

So I was at Starbucks debating between whole and two percent when I heard my name—*Sandy? Sandy!*—and I glanced over and there she was, Andra Rodriquez, all six-feet of her always-tanned body. We gave little shouts like we were actually happy to see one another. There were a few *God-you-look-greats* and *please-I'm-a-mess-so-why-don't-you-compliment-me-once-more's*. I obviously went with skim with her standing over my shoulder.

It'd been three years since I'd seen Andra, probably not since Caitlyn's wedding. We sat, our quick smiles masking the fact we had nothing to say. I knew Andra was still doing the whole model/actress thing, which was sad, now being what...thirty-six? Sure, she'd had some success on the outermost fringe of television, but really it was the roles of dead hookers and whatnot. I almost felt bad for her. I mean, she was like the one person from high school who even had a shot of doing something remotely resembling a dream. A Mexican father so she had that amazingly thick hair and cheekbones like implanted walnuts, but not too much, you know, a white mom so she didn't look Mexican, just *ethnic*. I knew shit was falling apart when I saw her in a deodorant commercial.

Andra told me she was home because her father was getting remarried. She asked what I was up to.

"I'm managing the Bebe at the mall," I said.

She responded to this with a pout, prompting me to remember that I'd always kind of hated her, inseparable in high school or not. I studied her then, her mouth pulled into a thin-lipped smile, and yeah, she still looked good, but you could tell LA had taken its toll. Like she had that look, beaten almost. Of course she was anorexic, always had been, but it was like it wasn't working anymore. Her jaw line was a hint swollen. Her skin looked like dried tobacco.

We sat there for a few minutes. She dropped names and I ate it up. She told me about a premier she'd attended the other night. She stopped talking. It wasn't midsentence, but close. She just kind of drifted off. Then those giant brown eyes of hers started to fill up. I touched her arm and asked what was wrong. She bit her lip. It was like we were transported twenty years back, us in the tenth grade, her crying because Jake got grabby after the homecoming game, all of us girls there consoling her, patting her back and petting her hair, us desperate to be close to greatness.

"Sandy," she said. "I went in for an audition. For a mom."

I smiled, told her there was no shame in that, thirty, flirty, and thriving, those kinds of things.

"They said I was too old," Andra said. "Too old for a toddler's *mom.*"

"What the fuck do they know?" I said. "I mean, everything's all *Teen Mom* and whatever. That's probably what they're looking for. Don't even sweat it. You look great. You'll get your big shot."

Andra wiped her eyes with the insides of her thumbs. Part of me was happy to see the Goddess of Stapleton High dashed like so many golden calves. And by *part*, I mean *all*, me with nothing but a failed marriage and a retail career somehow coming out as the victor.

It annoyed me when Andra regained some semblance of composure. She smiled. I thought about all the smiles she'd given boys and teachers and our fathers back in school, how this flashing of white from that caramel skin was like a never-denied electronic key, green means go and take whatever you want.

We stood. She told me she loved me and to stay in touch. I could've wrapped my arms around her twice. I tried not to imagine what she was thinking with her arms around me.

⋮

The next time I saw Andra, it was on TV, maybe eleven months after running into her at Starbucks. Jared, the guy I was dating (5'10", 170ish, brown hair, butt chin, decent shoulders) was flipping through the channels. I'd hated this about my ex-husband, Daniel, and hated it even more about Jared. That's when I saw her. I told Jared to turn it back. He did. There was Andra. She looked great. Like better than she had at senior prom when she'd worn that strapless champagne dress.

"Holy shit," I said. "I know her."

"Yeah?"

"She's like my best friend."

"Never heard you mention any famous friend before."

"Shut up."

I grabbed the remote and tried to turn up the volume, but the batteries were almost shot, so I had to walk to the TV. The closer I got to the screen, the better she looked. Like amazing. So young, so skinny. Radiant. Glowing. Everything. I knelt by the TV. The show was about a high-school vampire. It was the pilot episode. Andra was cast as the female lead, a fucking high-school girl. Somehow, she was able to pull it off; she looked that good. About halfway through, Andra's character, Maria Jones, was necking with some quarterback stud underneath the bleachers. Her fangs shot out. She ripped apart his neck, blood everywhere as she suckled. She dropped his limp body to the dirt. She said, "Sorry, I know how you hate a hickey."

I let Jared have sex with me that night because that's all we really did besides drink and watch TV. Sometimes while getting jackhammered, I would try to imagine what we had having any longevity. I'd think about it being different from my first marriage, this one full of passion and good times, this one like friends who fucked and friends who loved without the constructs of moral superiority. That night, I thought of these things, and they all felt like lies. I thought about Andra as Maria Jones ripping apart that high school boy's throat. I squeaked out a surprise orgasm while wondering what she'd done to look so good.

⋮

Varsity Vamps became a big deal, as you all know. The teenyboppers loved it because they knew all about popularity being a manifestation of evil. Their mothers loved it because Andra as Maria Jones was anti-sex. Their fathers loved it because Andra gave them all hard dicks.

After about a month of watching, I decided to give Andra a call. I wanted to congratulate her, to tell her I'd always known she could do it. But that's bullshit. Really, I wanted to know how she looked so amazing. Jared was over. I tried to feign an air of nonchalance: *I'm just stepping out to give Andra a ring.* He didn't seem very impressed, but he probably was. He probably told his realtor buddies that his girlfriend was besties with Maria Jones from *Varsity Vamps.* They would be like *no way, man, you gonna' work that into a little threesome action?* and Jared would grin because he was a simple man.

I sat on the top of the three steps leading to my condo. It's one of those places that tries to look hip and modern but is really just a row house with angular windows. It's the worst place in Stapleton besides the Section 8 housing behind me. From my front door, I can see the house Daniel and I built. He doesn't live there anymore. The money we made from selling afforded me this little slice of hell in the singles and poor-ish corridor of this wretched suburb.

I found Andra's name and hit *call.* It rang. It rang again. I knew she wasn't going to answer. *Varsity Vamps* had just ended. They probably all got together—the cast, the directors, the shady men with money who weren't credited—all of them together in some loft overlooking The Valley. The windows would be entire walls. It would be catered with jumbo shrimp. People would be cutting lines with American Express Centurion Cards. Maybe that was how Andra looked so skinny, a nice little habit? I doubted it; the people I knew who went down that road looked like they'd been beaten by bags of dicks. The phone rang again. Then she answered.

"Sandy, what's up?!"

"Hey, girl." I wasn't sure why I'd called her *girl.* I felt nervous, my natural reaction to any interaction with Andra.

"Everything okay?"

"What? Yeah, no, everything's good. Really good."

I sat there with the phone pressed to my ear. I couldn't think of a way to bridge the gap between a random call and asking how she'd turned back her clock fifteen years. But that's untrue. I knew, because women know these things, sisterly help only bartered through the currency of flattery. But I *really* didn't want to tell her how amazing she looked. How I enjoyed the show. How I knew she would make it. How even at thirty-six, she still looked like she was seventeen. I thought about us as juniors and us both trying out for the lead for Maria in the *West Side Story,* about how she received the part and I got Pauline, about how I'd called after the roles were posted to tell her I was happy for her, that I knew she would do a great job.

But I did.

Back in high school and sitting outside on the phone.

Because she was popular and beautiful and compliments were easier than silent confrontations and because just like as kids, she had something I wanted.

"Thank you," she said.

"I'm so proud of you," I said.

"You're the best, Sandy, you really are."

I figured I'd sucked her asshole enough to move on. I said, "How'd you...what'd you do to look so...I mean, you look amazing."

"Just rededicated myself to the craft," Andra said. "I started eating only raw foods, working out with an amazing trainer..."

I quit listening because her shit was rehearsed. That's the way it had always been with her.

"...and I don't know, I guess all the hard work paid off, you know?"

"That's great, that's really great."

Then we were quiet because we lived in different worlds.

"Thank you," she said.

"No, sorry, I should've called sooner."

"No, for always being there."

I could see into the yard of our old house. They'd put up a hideous screened-in porch, evidently thinking they were facing Bolivian-levels of malaria infection. The dutiful husband grilled burgers. Their toddler daughter was a chubby mess. The wife looked suicidal. I wondered how long it'd be until he stopped drinking and she couldn't, until he started using God to justify adultery.

"I'm going to send you something," Andra said.

"No, I don't need money or anything—"

"It's not money. It's a present. I think you'll like it."

"Um, okay. You really don't—"

"I know that. But I want to."

Slim-Me™. It was a bottle the size of a shot glass, red, almost appearing hand-blown. The only writing on it was the title, no nutritional facts, no *Made in China*, no directions or expiration date or price. Andra had written a note: *Enjoy!!!*

I held the vial. It was a bitchy thing to do, Andra sending me some diet drink. Like yeah, I'd put on a few pounds, but who hadn't? It was just like her. Fronting as a caring friend, but really, underneath that rehearsed pep—Andra cheering us along in high school, suggesting soft tones to bring out the green in our eyes, sending me this Slim-Me™—was really just her unsaid declaration: *Maybe this will help you not be so fucking average.*

But the old curiosity was stoked. I searched Google. There was nothing. No blogs. No distributors. No scandalous articles about actresses ingesting these bottles like so many pre-shoot enemas. Nothing. I rubbed its almost-smooth surface. *Fuck Andra.* I tossed it in my purse and went to work.

I work at the mall and yes, it's retail, and yes, I had once been a CPA before depression and before Daniel's indiscretions and before drinking became the only way I didn't blow my brains out, and yes, I sometimes eat lunch at the food court, and yes, the store is Bebe, but I am a *manager* and I leave my work at the mall so whatever, right? A job is a job is a job.

Being August, our fall line was coming in. Me and two other girls were setting up the front-left display. This is the most important part of the store. Studies show that when people walk in, they turn left, so I'm a stickler for beauty and perfection in our front-left displays, our mannequins holding just the right poses, wearing just the right thing. That particular day, we were striving for the *Am I going to the gym or am I comfortable in my walk of shame* type of look with some new velour jumpsuits.

The two girls helping me were both young, both still in college, or at least college-aged. I figured they knew things I didn't. Trendy things, like about certain drugs, certain diets, certain small vials of Slim-Me™. So I dropped it into conversation: "You guys heard about that Slim-Me?"

"Slim Fast?"

"No, Slim-Me, you know, like in that little red bottle?"

"Never heard of it," one said.

The other said, "I don't do any of that toxic diet stuff. Gluten free and spin are the way to go."

I nodded. I wanted to tell her that the herpes-concealing patch on her lip was not, in fact, herpes-concealing.

We finished with the display. The store didn't open for another twenty. The two girls talked about a new club. They said it was twenty-one plus but they had fakes. I wanted to die. The girls reminded me of Andra and myself years ago. I couldn't stand hearing them blabber on so gave them a ten, telling them to go grab me a latte, not specifying what type of milk, hoping they opted for whole so it would be a free-lapse.

They left.

Truth be told, I wanted to try on the cocktail dress we'd just gotten into the store. It was called the Silver Bullet. I was probably past the days when silver worked, but oh well. Like a girl can dream. Jared had invited me to some sort of party, something for the Independent Realtors of Colorado. The event was being held at The Brown Palace, so I figured it would be fancy. He'd asked and I'd said yes. He'd asked, and I'd thought it was a big step, relationship-wise, one I wasn't sure I wanted to make. I'd tried on the thought about us being three years down the road and us married, Jared holding the door for me, his hand on the small of my back as he guided me around to this person, that person, his hand after a few drinks sliding two inches lower, pinching my ass or maybe just letting it rest there as he whispered into my ear that I looked so good he had to *take* me in the bathroom, and maybe we could be one of those couples, one that did fun shit after marriage. Maybe one who others would for once want to be.

The eight was too small. I wasn't about to be the heifer in the ten so I made it work, telling myself Jared could zip me up. Standing there in the dressing room, the florescent lights illuminating everything I hated (my thighs, my calves, my pouch, my ass, my ankles, my neck, my tits that had even been saggy in high school). I looked like a tinsel Christmas tree ornament. But one that never makes it out of the cardboard box and onto the tree because it's fucking ugly. I tried to take the Silver Bullet off because it was pathetic, me in a dress meant for intern-aged girls trying to fuck Creative Directors, me wiggling out of its tentacle-like grasp, bits of flesh poking through my unzipped back. I thought of Andra sending me that vial. Maybe she wasn't trying to be a bitch? Maybe it was her admitting she'd used it because she'd needed help too. I liked that line of reasoning, that Hollywood was all taking it, that it was no big deal. I thought about everything my life had become: watching television with Jared and seeing that as having any staying power; being at least a decade older than all of my employees. I wouldn't have to tell Andra I took it. I reached into my purse. I took a tentative sip. It tasted like black licorice. I drank the rest.

⋮

There was diarrhea. There was sweat. There was a fever. This went on all night. Jared was at my place and he fetched me a cold washcloth and spread it over my closed eyes. I promised him or God or my ex-husband or myself that I'd be a better person if the pain stopped: I'd quit drinking; I'd write thank-you notes; I'd return Daniel's emails; I'd even get reinstated as a CPA. I must have been delirious because when that cold cloth hit my face, I told Jared I loved him.

⋮

The next morning, I awoke to Jared's lumbering snores. I had that confused panic of when you drink way too much and either tell your boss *Fuck you* or that *You want to fuck him*. My eyes fluttered open. I expected the most heinous hangover, because that had evidently become a thing once I hit thirty, but there was nothing, or rather, just the opposite: I felt like a goddamn preteen with lubricated joints and a hint of excitement about life.

I sprang (yes, *sprang*) out of bed and rushed to the bathroom. I stared in the mirror. I lifted my tank. My pouch, my constant companion since I'd grown hips in the fifth grade, was gone. I pulled down my flannel pajamas bottoms; the off-purple dimples colonizing my ass had vanished. Then I was naked studying myself and my thighs were tight and my face was perfectly sunken and my calves and ankles actually separated. I stood on the glass-plated scale. I couldn't stop laughing; I'd lost eleven pounds.

I rushed out of the bathroom. Jared woke up, wetting his sleep-dried mouth. He motioned for me to join him in bed. I didn't budge, just stood there and let him look, take me in, this woman so close to a girl, the new me I'd always known would one day rise from the ashes of my burnt down life. Jared must've noticed the improvements, because he grinned, telling me to get in bed that instant. I rubbed where my pouch had resided. I thought about his disgusting mouth touching my new body. I told him I was running late.

The little girls at work noticed right away because a woman can't shed a pound without the scrutiny/jealousy of the entire sisterhood. I told them I was only eating raw foods and working out with a personal trainer.

During one of my breaks, I slipped into the dressing room. The eight of the Silver Bullet was huge, the six no problem, the four fit but wasn't quite tight enough along my ass. I wrestled my way into the two. It was snug, but shit, I'd never worn a two. Never. Not even in high school when Andra and I kept designated Bic pens to jam down our throats in the bathroom after every meal. As soon as puberty hit, I went from little girl to woman, my ass and hips ready for bearing children. My pouch showed up at the same time, evidently my body worried about being stranded on some arctic sheet of ice for two-to-three weeks. But those were gone, *almost* gone. Truth be told, the meat on my hips was a bit much. I turned this way and that inside of that dressing room. I put the Silver Bullet on and took it off and put it on again. I rubbed my thighs, which were a world above what they'd once been, but were still a touch thick. Another inch on each one and I'd fit in that two, no prob.

⋮

That week, we watched *Varsity Vamps*. Andra as Maria Jones was taking a bath. It was a network show so of course her girl parts were covered with bubbles, which didn't stop Jared from having to cross his legs). Maria Jones had a few candles lit. This relaxing ritual was her reward for another foe defeated, another test aced, another boy's attempts at getting into her pants thwarted. But she didn't know about the werewolves circling her house. *We* did. There were four of them, two boys and two girls, coming from the neighboring subdivision, their attack mirroring the upcoming homecoming football game. Finally, Maria Jones' sixth sense kicked in. She stealthily turned off the faucet with her toes so she could better hear.

Jared laughed. He said, "Your friend's got some big ol' feet."

Later that night, I told Jared I was going on a walk. This wasn't a normal practice, athletic exertion somewhat of an allergen to me, but he was watching *Sports Center*, so he gave his autopilot response of *sounds good, babe.* I walked across the street that separated people who were happy to be in Stapleton from us rejects who had to deal with the boisterous noise of TGIF. I couldn't stop thinking about Andra as Maria Jones slipping into that tub; there was no extra inch on *her* hips. And that's all I needed, an inch, maybe two, one more bottle of Slim-Me™. I imagined the size two of the Silver Bullet slipping on like a silk camie. I called Andra.

She picked up on the fourth ring.

"My God, where'd you find that stuff?"

Andra laughed. It was a beautiful laugh, rehearsed, somehow effortless. I pictured her in the high school cafeteria with her head tilted back, that ethnic hair falling from her face, all of us watching, listening, mimicking, trying in vain to experience the world with as much gaiety.

"Thought you might enjoy it," Andra said.

"It's like, God..."

"Something like that."

"Where can I get another?"

Andra didn't say anything for a few seconds. The five minutes of walking caused my feet to ache. I knelt down and rubbed what was looking like the beginnings of a bunion.

"I'll pay," I said. "I'm not looking for another kickback or anything."

"It's not that."

"Then what?"

"It's just...I don't know. Like nobody knows what's actually in it. Nobody knows if it's safe."

"It could be heroin for all I care. I feel amazing. Look pretty decent, too."

"There might be consequences," Andra said. "Like unintended ones."

"Yeah, I got pretty sick, but whatever, right?"

"I guess."

"Then what the fuck, girl, hook a bitch up." I tried to raise my voice like I was joking.

Silence.

"Andra?"

"Your feet. I think it makes your feet grow."

"Feet?" I said, laughing.

"Forever. They keep growing *forever.*"

"Who the hell cares about feet?"

"Sandy, stop."

"What is it? A couple hundred? Five? Like it's not a problem. I'll send you a check right now."

"Just trust me."

"Andra, don't be like this. Like one more is all I'm asking."

"Sandy..."

I bit my lip and clenched everything. When I opened my eyes, I realized I was standing in front of the house Daniel and I had built. The new owner's fat kid had drawn all over the sidewalk with pastel chalk. I heard children playing in the alley. There were so many minivans. All of the lawns were immaculate because the HOA was run by a man who probably idolized Hitler. I thought about still living there with Daniel. I imagined agreeing to go along to his first AA meeting. I envisioned myself having quit drinking. We would've had a child because that was the fear, that I couldn't or didn't want to stop, that I'd be an unfit mother ripe for a Lifetime melodrama. I wondered if a child would've made things better or worse or if it would've prevented Daniel from cheating or if I'd have been capable of change or at least capable of love.

"Sandy?"

I imagined Andra sitting in some penthouse eating fresh mangos and her signing autographs at Comic-Con and her on red carpets and her as Maria, both in *Varsity Vamps* and in *West Side Story*. This was another example of her giving me an inch but never the whole thing. Never her full attention. Never her full friendship. Never running the risk of being up-staged. Never really caring about what I was doing or what guys made me happy or that my marriage had blown the fuck apart and I was now living in the shadow of the Caucasian American Dream, or maybe it was just a continuation of living in Andra's shadow, tall and dark and mysterious like her complexion, me so happy for any chink of light that leaked through, me just wanting to matter.

"Fuck you," I said.

"What?"

"No, really, like this power play. That's what it is. You know it. Like you always have to be better and—"

"Stop."

"No, *you* stop. You know I'm right. You always have to be the best. Back in high school and now. Always."

I wiped my eyes. She probably did the same thing two thousand miles away.

The front door opened. The behemoth of a toddler squinted her eyes and cocked her head. *Was she scared? Did she think I was a monster? Was this the first moment when she understood there were differences between women, the us's and the them's, the skinny and the fat, those who believed things would work out and those who knew differently?*

I spoke into the phone: "I'm sorry. I need one more. That's it. Tell me how much to send you."

"I don't need your money."

⋮

The bottle arrived two days later. There wasn't a note that time, just the bottle cocooned in bubble-wrap. I called Jared and told him I felt a migraine coming on. He asked what he could do; did I want some soup? Some company? Somebody to place a cold washcloth on my head? I told him I was fine. I told him I'd see him on Saturday for the party. He told me he loved me. I hung up.

I thought about the licorice-tasting liquid mutating cells, causing growths, blocking valves, burrowing into fleshy membrane walls. I thought about it leading to heart failure or kidney failure or liver failure. I thought about my feet growing maybe a half-size larger. I thought about the single spotlight on Andra in our high school spring play, how even the seniors watching knew she was a better Maria than me. I put the vial to my lips. I was so close, another inch on either hip.

Cramps and vomiting and fever blisters and what felt like bone spurs burrowing into each of my ten toes.

Six AM rolled around. I couldn't wait to look at myself in the mirror. My skin hugged my hipbones. I cried because I looked beautiful, felt something close to that.

That day at work, one of the girls pulled me aside. She was just a little kid, blonde, gravity still an intellectual concept for her. She asked me what was going on.

I tilted my head back, letting the hair fall away from my face, and laughed.

"Serious," she said. "We're all getting worried."

"It's this new raw diet. You should try it."

"That's bullshit," she said.

I smiled. I said, "Jealousy's an ugly color on you."

I swam in the two.

The zero fit like a wetsuit. I was beyond fuckable. At lunch, I went to Nordstrom's for a pair of shoes because none of mine were close to fitting (a small price to pay for perfection). I picked out a pair of Jimmy Choos with a silver bow across the toes. I gave myself some wiggle room, upping my regular size by one, asking the teenage sale's associate for a nine. She returned with the shoes. I told her I was all good, not wanting her there to see my feet. She didn't catch the hint. She gasped when I took off my shoes. My toes were man fingers, bruises abounding, a touch of blood. I pretended this was normal. I jammed my foot into the Jimmy Choo. There was at least two inches of heel that wouldn't even slip into the pump. I asked if they ran small. She shook her head, said they actually ran a touch big. I talked about being on my feet all day and the humidity and then I said I was pregnant and that must be the reason for the swelling. She bought out the biggest pair they had, a thirteen. They were half my monthly mortgage. I used a credit card, one with twenty-two percent interest.

⋮

That week, Maria Jones was trying to be Good Vampire. Over the season, she'd developed a sense of morality. She declared she would no longer feed on humans. By the end of the hour, she was so malnourished, so skinny, sick, bones and ribs and those big brown eyes dug inches into her skull, she relented. She went to a nursing home and found the most senile woman in the whole ward. The old lady had one line: *help me.*

Maria Jones put her out of her misery.

I snorted a laugh, thinking that was totally Andra, her believing her actions were so fucking saintly.

⋮

The night of the party, Jared said *Goddamn.* That's it. He stood in my tiny kitchen. He looked about as handsome as he could in his Men's Warehouse suit. I ran my hands over his chest, straightening his light blue tie. I pecked the dimple of his chin. I said, "Goddamn, yourself."

He popped for valet. He took my arm. It wasn't a red carpet or anything, but the entrance had a carpeted runner leading up the four steps. The party was in a small banquet room. An ice sculpture of a house with a *"For Sale"* sign staked in front served as a centerpiece for the buffet table. There were shrimp around its base. Maybe three hundred people milled about. Jared told me he was going to get us drinks. I told him I wanted champagne.

We walked around the party. Jared introduced me to fellow realtors. I smiled at wives, winked at husbands, more than once letting my grasp linger for a suggestive second. A DJ spun songs from our formative years, *Boys to Men* and the like. It felt like high school. But it was different, because I wasn't standing in the shadow of Andra. No, *I* was for once the spot-lit beacon, people's stares so greedy for inclusion. I laughed beautiful laughs. My hair draped effortlessly. I shook my shoulders on the more pronounced downbeats. Jared was at my side, a disposable accessory.

At one point, he leaned over and whispered in my ear *we need to get you out of that condo.* I wasn't sure what this comment was in reference to. Maybe he knew it was depressing being in view of the happy family occupying the house I'd built? Maybe this was his way of asking me to move in with him? I drank my fourth glass of champagne. I wondered if this was his not-so-subtle precursor to marriage. I laughed a little, Jared thinking he was good enough, that I'd really be okay with his growing widow's peak, his tired stories about deals that didn't come together, his reenactments of triples he hit in softball games. *Had he seen me lately?* I moved an inch away, his hand sliding off the exposed skin of my back. He winked. Such a simple man.

All around me were tacky dresses and fake smiles and hair-sprayed bangs and love handles and pouches and thick thighs and elephant skin arms. The house ice sculpture melted, its yard filled with gnawed shrimp tails like so many discarded kids' toys. I was the skinniest woman at the party. My feet killed. I stood in the middle of three hundred people. Songs played from decades past. I thought about Andra, her little fifteen minutes with *Varsity Vamps*. The show would maybe have one more season before it was cancelled. She couldn't look like a teenager forever, with or without Slim-Me™. She'd eventually take the role of a mother with teenage children. Her shit was bound to fall apart; beauty's function was to impregnate the beholder. I smiled. Jared thought this grin was directed at him. He tried to give me bedroom eyes. I knew he wanted to *take* me in the bathroom.

I drank more champagne, still looking at all the women—the fours, the eights, the tens, the few pathetic twelves—and they were all giving polite laughs at the shoulders of their paunchy husbands. I imagined these women getting ready, squeezing into three-year-old dresses, complaining nothing fit, their husbands telling them they looked fine—*no, I mean* great, *baby*—and they probably all had stood in the bathroom mirror studying themselves, everything they hated, their flabby triceps, their saddlebags, their gunts, their self-hatred only compounded by the knowledge that there'd be a woman at the party who fit effortlessly into a zero, somebody their husbands couldn't help but introduce themselves to, somebody whose shadow they could never outgrow.

But then I noticed these women weren't staring. They weren't even sneaking glances from behind tilted champagne flutes. I tried to make my laughs louder, my movements more pronounced. Jared asked what was so funny. I thought about Andra walking into the party. About how she would have to pay for her drinks at the cash bar. About how the only appetizers were already-devoured shrimp. About it being in Colorado.

About it being filled with average people who would return to their average homes and kiss their average children before having average sex on their average mattresses inside of their average houses in average subdivisions built around the ideal of the average being something to celebrate.

I remembered how hard I'd prayed for that part back in high school, Maria in the *West Side Story*. I'd never wanted anything more, practicing "I Feel Pretty" for a month straight, me in the shower singing into the iron-rich water, my hands kneading my just-visible pouch. I remembered standing offstage in the school auditorium. I'd cried watching Andra as Maria, her alone, her singing "I Feel Pretty", her voice the perfect inflection of confidence and vulnerability, me not knowing if this was a blessing or a curse, a statement or a question.

Jared whispered I was the sexiest girl there. I winced from the pain of my new bunion. I looked at him—his butt chin, his bushy eyebrows, his thinning hair, his smirk—and I knew I'd go home with him that night. That he would penetrate me while thinking of someone else. That I would eventually agree to sell my condo. That we would cohabitate. That he'd pressure me to cut down on my drinking so we could have a child. That part of me would want this—had *always* wanted this—because I'd always imagined the front steps of my suburban home to have the colorful doodles of my daughter's chalk. I knew that I'd push him away because certain people don't get things they want. I knew that Andra would never step foot in this gala. I knew that nights like this would be as close to greatness as I'd ever reach.

Excavation

We were at the doctor because Hailey's breath was beyond bad. The smell was like death, and not just in the mornings, mind you, but a constant, my wife's halitosis. It was eating at the dinner table, jostling for position as we brushed our teeth, tucking our daughter in at night, even talking on the phone, that meaty aroma somehow seeping through whatever magical wavelength cells operated on.

Our daughter, Ellie, is three. One day, she pointed to Hailey's mouth and said, "Mama, dirty diaper."

Hailey thought it was cancer. Cancer of the throat. Cancer of the tonsils. Maybe some sneaky cancer residing between her gums and molars. But she thinks everything is cancer; her mother and father both met their premature demises via the breasts and prostate, respectively.

"It's not cancer."

"You don't know that."

"It's not cancer."

"Then I'm just disgusting."

"You're not disgusting."

I took off early from work and accompanied Hailey to the doctor. Why? Because I'm a good guy, and she was certain she was about to receive a death sentence starting with a C. The doctor's office was small with all the usual things. Hailey sat on the little table covered in white paper, which crinkled under her nervous movements. I exuded calmness. I talked about things that didn't matter. She told me to shut up. I smiled, one I hoped conveyed how silly this whole thing was, as well as how much I loved her.

Hailey suffers from anxiety, usually revolving around death. This fear is pretty nondiscriminatory with its subjects, but if I had to guess, a map of her fear would be an earthquake diagram with Ellie at its epicenter. The anxiety is new, or *new-ish*, life and circumstance teaming up with the back-to-back deaths of her parents and then the birth of our daughter, so much sadness and so many hormones altering the woman she'd been. People don't know this about her. They think she's beautiful, her eyes like semi-finished jade and a body that isn't fair for having birthed a child. She's funny. She's smart. She makes a living trafficking in empathy, counseling at-risk youth for Denver Public Schools, and she's a good enough person to enjoy it.

The doctor finally came in. He was old with a gobble for a chin. Hailey struggled through small talk. I knew she just wanted a diagnosis. The doctor used a light and tongue depressor. He didn't wear a mask, but I bet he wanted one.

Hailey gagged on the Popsicle stick. The doctor used a giant Q-Tip and scraped the back of her throat, causing her to gag even more. She squeezed my hand.

"It's not cancer," the doctor said.

Her hand relaxed. She sighed. Then she squeezed again. She asked, "What is it?"

"It's tonsilloliths, more commonly known as tonsil stones."

"Tonsil stones?"

"It's really no big deal," the doctor said. He threw the wooden stick into the trash. "Just bits of food and bacteria getting caught in the recesses of your tonsils. Mix in some white blood cells, and you get little stones."

"You're sure?" Hailey said.

"Positive. It's nothing to be alarmed over." He touched her shoulder. He told her to gargle with warm saltwater three times a day. He said she could use the ginormous Q-Tips—handing her a few—to try to excavate any particularly bothersome stones.

We left. We held hands walking to our cars. It was a nice enough afternoon and I felt pretty good about things. Hailey must've as well, because she turned to face me, snagging my belt loops with her fingers.

"So...do you *really* have to go back to the office?"

I knew what she was getting at. I held my breath, giving her a quick peck on the cheek. I told her I'd have to take a rain check.

⋮

It's my duty to drop Ellie off at daycare. It's probably the highlight of my day. We talk on the drive; she tells me about kids she's in love with and kids who are mean. I tell her the mean kids are unhappy and trying to bring everyone else down. I don't really watch the road, but instead look at my daughter in the rearview mirror. She's big, 99% across the board. Kids haven't yet started calling her fat, but I know it's coming, which breaks my heart.

I hug her and tell her I love her more than anything. I usually drive around for a half hour even though Allstate is only five minutes away, thus the reason we'd chosen Bright Horizons Daycare. We'd had a lot of those talks while trying to get pregnant the first go around, the pre-battle plans about being an involved father, a presence in her life, unlike my father, our bodies sweaty and Hailey's breath not yet rotten, us talking about two kids, camping trips and summer barbeques and Christmases spent in a cabin we would some day own. We'd had plenty of time for those conversations, fourteen months to be exact. Evidently, Hailey had a tilted uterus. We even made an appointment at a fertility clinic, but finally got pregnant, probably the happiest day of my life.

My office is in a strip mall. Our neighbor to the west is Subway, which makes our office smell like yeast. It's a horrible place, one nobody ever sets out to work in, but money is money and health care is health care. I smile at my coworkers, the people who tell me about Johnny's double in Little League, those who ask if I'd caught last night's episode of *The Office—Man, it's like we* are *that show*—and I'm all smiles, all *Wow, a double!*, and *Please, Dunder Mifflin has nothing on Allstate.*

The morning after Hailey's doctor appointment, I sat at my cubicle. I put in my earpiece, which, when I thought about it, had a certain resemblance to the Q-Tips the doctor had given Hailey. I'd fallen asleep the previous night to the sound of her gagging and spitting from the bathroom, only to be woken up at some point past midnight. I'd remembered the rain check with a hardening of my penis. She thrust the Q-Tip in my face, saying *I got one, I got one.*

The smell was church reception parlors and hot garbage. I could see a white chunk the size of a Number Two pencil eraser.

She set the Q-Tip with its booty on the nightstand, delicate as if it were a humming bird hatchling. She straddled me. She said *it's time*. She must have been fertile. I'm no masochist, so I avoided her mouth by kissing her neck. Luckily, we made love on our sides. I could smell the stone, either the one drying out on the nightstand or the ones still lodged in her throat. I buried my face in her hair in attempts to huff the vanilla of her shampoo. I told her I was getting close. Normally, she'd tell me to slow my roll, maybe guide my head below the sheets for a few in order to get her a mere thrust away from coming, but that's more of a sex-for-climax maneuver, and we were in a sex-for-insemination scenario, so she told me to *blast it good*.

I blasted it as well as I knew how.

Allstate Insurance, this is Josh...

I'm supposed to sell an average of four policies a day. At one point, I was able to accomplish this goal, thus affording us twenty-percent down on our home. That was before. I'm not sure what the *before* is in relation to, only that I'm firmly now entrenched in the *after*. I am lucky to sell one policy per day.

Most people's numbers are down over the summer because men are happier and women are too busy with their children to be bothered by solicitors. But my numbers are bottom of the barrel. Last week, I sold a single life insurance policy. The woman was thirty-three years old, the same age as myself, a commonality I used to my advantage, veering off from my usual script, telling her that yeah, we were still young, still had the best years of our lives ahead of us, *God willing* (Christian talk soothes most people), but it was the responsible thing to do. I told her I had a five-hundred-thousand-dollar policy on myself. I said, "Maybe it's a bit much, but when I think about my amazing wife and beautiful daughter—"

"How old?"

"Just turned three."

"Mine just turned one."

"Walking yet?"

"Getting into everything."

"Isn't that the truth?"

I could hear the woman smile. I had her. I said, "When I think about them, I realize there's no monthly expense too great."

She told me she knew it was something she should do, but money was *so* tight at the moment.

I told this lady accidents happen. Tragedies. I told her things didn't always go as planned. I said, "We need to be prepared. It's an act of love."

⋮

Our neighborhood is like TV and the movies and it's in the suburbs and there are three styles of houses that alternate in a little line down evenly spaced blocks. Ours is garage front-right, porch back-left. This is Stapleton, Colorado. This is the result of Clinton economics and it is the entire country and this is us sitting in our screened-in porch (a costly addition, but Hailey insisted, so certain some snake or insect was going to kill our daughter) and Ellie is serving her stuffed animals dinner even though we already ate. Hailey is nursing a cup of hot water filled with salt. We are talking about work. I lie, say I'm looking good for commission this month. Hailey tells me about one of the students she counsels at the high school, how this girl is lost, broken, first by fathers, then by boys, then by drugs. She says there's nothing she can do. She says it's devastating to realize everything she does is pointless. Mosquitoes search for blood outside of our screens. This is every night.

⋮

Hailey has a period tracker on her phone. It tells her when PMS will rear its ugly head, when The Red will flow, when she is fertile. This application is the Bible of our lives. Those few days of perfect soil are like The Sermon on the Mount and we bless the meek in every conceivable position—the other day Hailey greeted me upside down, resting on her neck and shoulder blades, balancing against the base of the bed with her legs like a capital Y—hoping against hope that gravity and downward thrusts and *blasting it good* would team up for a successful alley-oop on her egg.

That month, PMS came in the form of a frowning face on Hailey's period tracker app. I checked it while she gargled saltwater. Her period came in the form of a stain in the shape of Louisiana on our sheets. She cried. I told her it was no big deal; the sheets were only from Target. I said I'd pick up the same ones. More cries. Different ones? Hailey didn't say anything. She didn't even get out of bed to put in a tampon.

It was around this time when I quit using my Breathe Rights for my snoring. It was a matter of self-preservation; the strips widen the nasal cavity, which made the smell even worse. I'd be lying in bed. My nose would be getting every bit of her decaying white blood cells, the chicken parmesan from two nights prior festering in the moist pockets of tonsil. I wasn't sure how much more I could take. But I didn't say anything because I'm a good guy. One night, I rested my hand on her tummy, which she called her blueberry muffin top. Underneath that tiny pouch was her moderately-to-severely tilted uterus. I wondered if anything would grow in there again. Hailey faced me. Her breath hit me before her words: "It's getting worse. I can taste it."

"No, I think it's letting up."
"Bullshit."
"I think the saltwater's helping."
"I'm fucking toxic."
"I love you."
"Toxic and barren."

      ⋮

The doctor said nothing else could be done, unless, of course, Hailey wanted to have her tonsils removed. I asked the HR woman at work with cheeks like ass implants if my insurance would cover the operation. She shook her head, saying unless it was doctor ordered, the removal of my wife's tonsils would be considered an *elective surgery.*

"You've got to be kidding me."

"Haven't kidded anyone in over a decade," she said.

"What? Why?"

"Life's about all the hilarity anyone can take in one sitting."

So we went to a holistic medicine place Hailey's sister swore by. I was expecting some sort of cross between an opium den and Whole Foods, but it was just a store in a strip mall. I was pretty sure it used to be a Blockbuster. Hailey chewed gum, two pieces at a time. She studied her phone. It must have been getting close to fertile soil.

A lady with an isosceles triangle of moles on her left cheek came out. She shook our hands. Her name was Dorothy. She didn't look like a Dorothy. Hailey talked with her mouth pretty much closed, as she'd mastered over the summer. We followed Dorothy to a back office.

There were diplomas framed on her wall so that made me feel a little less ripped-off. Dorothy asked about the stones. Hailey said they were getting worse; she could feel them back there growing and festering. Dorothy never let her eyes fall away from Hailey's. I liked this about her, the way she nodded like she really understood and felt compassion. I'd rented *Bambi* for Ellie in this very store and she'd cried because she was too young to understand things died.

"When did they start to worsen?" Dorothy asked.

"About three months ago."

"Have there been any changes to your diet?"

"No."

"Any additional stressors?"

"No."

I looked over at Hailey, who seemed rigid then, determined to ignore my gaze.

"Okay," Dorothy said.

I cleared my throat. Hailey gave me a look like I'd just stabbed our daughter. There were smiles all around. Then silence. So much of our lives were taking place in the quiets of bitten tongues.

"The body is a strange mechanism," Dorothy said. "It always seeks a balance, an equilibrium. Sometimes physical manifestations of emotional issues present themselves. The throat, the portal to the fourth chakra, it usually deals in the realm of *withholding*."

"Is it cancer?"

"No, Mrs. Hudson, it is not cancer."

"Is there a cure?"

"We can treat the *symptoms*."

"Okay, let's do that."

⋮

My only sale of August was to a forty-nine-year-old teacher. He told me he was a grandfather now. He realized it was time. I went through all of the questions. He paused when I asked about smoking. A few minutes later he coughed a moving-the-armoire-across-a-wooden-floor cough so I marked *yes* and his monthly premium went up seventy-nine dollars but I didn't care because he was a liar.

Hailey on top. Hailey on all-fours. Hailey sideways and Hailey in the bathtub and Hailey drinking her prescribed aloe-peppermint-cayenne tea and Hailey taking her temperature and what about me? I was simply the guy depositing his ejaculate into the vagina of his wife. That's what it felt like. I wanted her to wear her one piece of lingerie. I wanted her to tell me I was sexy. For her to light candles and for her to not smell and for her to say *why are we doing this?* But I kept pumping to her demands—*deeper, blast it, deeper*—because I'm a good guy.

Hailey on her iPhone. Hailey calling in sick to work. Hailey not getting out of bed. Hailey telling Ellie to leave her alone.

No, I missed the last episode of *The Office.*

Wow, Johnny went three for three?

Allstate Insurance, this is Josh...

One night I grilled burgers. We didn't really like hamburgers, but with a backyard, I felt like a grill was something I'd needed. I'd gone to Lowe's. I'd been up-sold because I am the kind of guy who usually lets this happen. It was big and red and had four burners and even a heating-stove on the right side for vegetables or something. One of my neighbors said it was a *mighty fine specimen.* I hadn't known what to say to that.

I grilled the burgers. Ellie set the table because we believe in trying to teach her responsibility. Hailey drank a beer, the first one in her past seven cycles.

"Here we go," I said. I doled out the patties.

"Thanks, honey."

"Thanks, Daddy."

"Anything for my girls."

Hailey passed the baked beans. Then the corn. She served Ellie.

"More."

"Why don't you eat this first, then you—"

"More."

"Ellie, we do not raise our voice in this family," I said.

We started with our meals.

Looking at my daughter eat like she'd never seen food before, I wondered how old a child had to be to sign up for soccer. Maybe Hailey was thinking the same thing. She was finally turning, seeing something not normal about our daughter's appetite, her weight, her bowling ball face, because Hailey was spaced out, staring. I followed her gaze to her hamburger with one bite missing. Grease and blood pooled in the small divot of her plate.

"Is something wrong?" I asked. I gave her arm a gentle squeeze.

She shook her head and it was blonde bangs over her eyes and Ellie saw this and started doing the same thing.

"Stop that," I told Ellie.

She didn't.

"Stop that, now."

She did.

The mosquitoes and the neighbors and the country went on living outside of our screened-in porch.

"What is it?" I asked.

Hailey took a swig of beer.

"Maybe it's you?" Hailey said.

Ellie was shaking her head again. The ends of her hair painted strokes in her ketchup.

I took another bite of my hamburger and wiped the blood off of my chin with a napkin, a cloth one with a pastel floral print. I wanted to tell Hailey it was bullshit, hurtful, her comment. It had worked before. It was her body, which was obviously toxic. Her tilted uterus. And then I thought about asking her if it would really fix a goddamn thing—shopping for gender-neutral one-pieces, converting her office into a nursery, watching TV on the couch with her between my arms, all twenty of our fingers on her belly, shielding our next child from the world outside, as if this was all we really needed, if this would be enough to make her quit obsessing over every conceivable way we were going to die—and I almost said these things, but she took another bite of her burger and then I did, too.

⋮

Two days later, I was at another doctor's office. He was mine, Dr. Stoltz, and had been for years. He asked how long we'd been trying. I said seven months. He jotted down a note. I told him it'd taken a long time before Ellie. He took another note. I told him about Hailey's tilted uterus. Pen to paper. He said the whole tilted uterus thing was a bit of an old wives' tale, not much science behind it affecting rate of insemination. The white paper crinkled underneath me. He apologized he didn't have any aides. I blushed and told him it was okay.

He left and I started to masturbate. I thought of one of Ellie's preschool teachers with her red hair and body like Irish rains. I imagined her freckled breasts in my face. Then I thought of Hailey and her commands and our foreplay being the checking of her period tracker and the taking of her temperature and her telling me to blast every drop inside of her. And then I thought of ten years before when I first saw her and it wasn't love at first sight because that doesn't happen, but maybe it was, love that is, Hailey in her little jean skirt and red halter and ponytail and the way she'd kept my stare like an invitation and how we'd been drunk and talked and I'd made her laugh and how we went to the bathroom and it was the best sex because everything was still yet to happen. I came into the cup the doctor had given me.

⋮

A woman of middle age said it was kind of messed up what I was doing. She said making money by playing off the fear of death, of leaving her loved ones not only motherless, but financially destitute, it was shitty of me.

"I have a five-hundred-thousand-dollar policy for myself."

"That's great."

"Because I *care*. Because it's the *responsible* thing to do."

"That's a crock of shit."

"Because I'm a—"

"Don't call me again."

⋮

A few days later, I picked up Ellie, smiling at her redheaded teacher. I hefted my daughter into the car seat and kissed her nose. She started to sing and kick the back of my seat.

My phone rang. It was Dr. Stoltz. He said, "Mr. Hudson, I have the results of your sample."

"Everything check out?"

"Not exactly."

"What? What do you mean?"

"I mean you have a very low sperm count. I'm sorry."

"Like how low?"

"Like low enough for insemination to be all but an impossibility."

Ellie sang louder and kicked harder.

"I don't understand," I said. "There's got to be...I mean, it obviously was high enough to work before."

Dr. Stoltz didn't respond. I realized this was his rebuttal, his saying without actually saying. Finally, he said, "Then I would thank whatever power you believe in because it was a miracle."

I didn't know how to respond or even if I was supposed to.

That night, I stood in the doorway and watched the two girls of my life. They both lay there on the bed, Hailey reading a story. Their yellow hair met on the same pillow. They were beautiful. Hailey seemed calm, un-anxious. I wanted them to extend an arm, an invitation. For a new baby to bridge the gap between us. They both looked up from the book. I imagined what I must look like to them: a strange man with dark hair, backlit and ominous, standing on the outskirts.

I poured myself a drink and sat in the screened-in porch. I thought about Googling causes for lowered sperm count, like tight boxer briefs or maybe low testosterone. I wondered if my count had always been subpar. I was scared of what I'd uncover. A moth fluttered against the mesh cage where I sat. I was kind of drunk. Hailey had insisted on the screened-in porch, so sure of innumerable outside threats. Ellie could be a giant because she wasn't mine. The hippie doctor had said the stones were a symptom of *withholding*. The silence of the backyard was deafening.

I walked back inside. Hailey was in the upstairs bathroom. She called my name. I thought maybe a pregnancy test showed a blue plus sign, so I rushed in, ready to embrace her and our new future. Hailey was in tears. Maybe I'm not always a good guy because my first thought was, *Get the fuck over your self-indulgent problems.*

"I can see it," Hailey said. "It's huge. *Huge.*"

"What?"

"The thing."

"The *what?*"

"The chunk. The stone."

"Oh."

I relaxed because it was only her toxic throat.

Hailey grabbed my arm. She said, "You have to get it out."

Her breath was worse than it had ever been.

"No."

"Please."

"Just use the Q-Tip thing."

"I can't get it. *Please.*"

She held onto my arms and her face looked older, not wrinkles, but just like she was tired, sick of everything. She begged, saying this one was the root of it all.

I told her to sit on the toilet. She did. I told her to tilt her head back. She did. I told her to open up. She did.

I could see the stone. It was the size of a penny, growing from her left tonsil. Its texture was moist bumps; its color curdled milk. I put the Q-Tip into her mouth and accidently jabbed her uvula. She gagged. We started over. I placed my hand around her throat for better purchase. I held my breath. I touched the stone with the instrument and she gagged so I flexed my hand around her throat because I was close. I pushed harder, ignoring the retching. I dug, but the stone wouldn't dislodge. I tried to think of an injury suffered over the past three years, some forgotten kick to the groin. Maybe my cellphone was too close to my testacies? Hailey flailed at my arms. I squeezed harder. I was so close. The stone was bigger than a penny, its depth deceptive, more like a marble. Blood pooled on her tongue. I almost had it. Ellie was fat and blonde and didn't have a single one of my physical characteristics or personality traits. It could've been as simple as Hailey paging through mug shots and saying *that one*, a quick doctor-administered *good blast* of another man's sperm inside of her, problem solved. Her flailing became clawing. Would it make a difference if Ellie weren't mine? I almost had the stone. Hailey kicked me. I squeezed and dug. She drooled blood onto my fingers. Ellie was the only daughter I would ever have. Hailey was moments away from losing consciousness. Anxiety was nothing but the inability to come to terms with death. I tried to make a living capitalizing on that fear, exploiting it. Maybe the only reason we were trying for another child was to stave off our decaying bodies. Miracles *did* happen, so fuck what Dr. Stoltz had said.

For some reason, I imagined a phone call from myself. I imagined being sold a life insurance policy. Allstate Me would get me talking about my family. He'd want to hear a smile in my voice. He'd want me to start making decisions based on emotion. He'd ask about my kids. I'd pause here, a catch I would have for the rest of my life, uncertainty, insecurity, shame. I'd push these thoughts aside. I'd tell Allstate Me I had one daughter, beautiful, the light of my life. He'd build rapport by hitting on the love of our children. Then he'd get me to admit I'd do anything in my power to ensure she had the best life possible. He'd hover over this statement, knowing he was close, but I still needed to see him as an alley instead of a salesman. He'd say *did you hear the one about the birthing pain transfer machine? Yeah, so this couple is delivering their baby, and the doc tells them he has a machine that can transfer the pain of childbirth over to the father. The husband says let's do it. The doc starts at 10%, and the husband surprisingly handles it really well. Up to 20%, no sweat. 50% he's still smiling. The doc zaps him with 100% and the baby pops out. All is well, but when the couple gets home, the postman is dead on their doorstep.* I would be laughing because to do anything else would be crushing. Allstate Me would say every comedy was rooted in tragedy; life about all the hilarity one could handle in a single sitting. He'd drop his tone, saying accidents happened, outside forces or sneaky twists of the body, nobody immune to devastation.

The stone rolled onto her tongue.

I let go.

She spit it onto the floor.

I knew I would never mention my test results to Hailey. I knew Hailey would eventually become impregnated again, and we'd cherish this miracle. We would each have the symptoms of withholding, the act of which was done out of love.

We both looked at this foreign substance on our Spanish tile. I ran my hand through Hailey's thin hair. And silly us, we actually thought we'd accomplished something.

The Beautician

There are two types of people in this world: pinky-winkies and frownie-brownies. This is a fact. Either your asshole is the color of healthy gums or your asshole is the color of a coffee-stained ceramic mug. There's no shame in being a frownie-brownie; it simply *is*.

How do I know this? For years, I was paid handsomely for bleaching anuses. My services were requested and I'd show up to rich people's homes and set up my table in seldom-used rooms and I'd dim the lights and get a few citronellas going and then I'd start with a massage because nobody wants to be FDAU without a little trust-building rapport and then it'd be onto the act in question, my battle against Father Time and diet and genetics and pigmentation as I'd transform FBs into PWs, as I'd give people new lives.

My name is Candace. If you must know, I'm a frownie-brownie by birth, but nobody, not even that hack Bridget at Bridget's Bleaching would be able to tell I've catapulted myself into the land of proud PWs.

You may also be wondering how, exactly, one gets into the field of anus beautification? Most of us stumbled into the business through waxing salons. Once Hollywood caught wind (pun mildly intended) of the practice adult stars were doing down in The Valley, they started requesting a remedy for their darkness. Word spread. Stories were printed. Women across the country read about this new form of betterment while waiting in Safeway lines, suddenly aware of their coloring for the first time, so many handheld mirrors in locked master bathrooms. So those women giving Brazilians had to learn to dab burning bleach.

That is not my story.

I'm a normal enough woman; I was a good enough kid. I moved from Illinois to Colorado for college (full academic ride), where I studied PR and marketing. Upon graduating, I was hired by Sports Authority (corporate). They started me at fifty-five, which was nothing to sneeze at.

I'm fairly attractive and fairly fun, so I enjoyed this part of my life. I embraced the whole *young professional* thing without even realizing I was doing it. I joined coed volleyball leagues and loved brunch and knew enough about craft beer and football to spike the interest of most Colorado boys. There were weekend trips to the mountains. There was a brief summer of road biking. Jazz in the Park, themed 5k runs, baseball games with the mountains offering up shade...I thought I had arrived.

Then I met Jared.

Jared was a touch older with nostrils like God spent the better part of a long weekend chiseling down to the nanoparticle. He owned a loft in Lo-Do and split a timeshare in Breckenridge. He wasn't exactly in my tightest grouping of friends, more like two Venn diagrams removed. I'd see him at bars and the occasional barbeque, Jared with his sockless topsiders and seersucker Polos, his easy grin, everyone vying for his attention. I figured he was way out of my league, which he was. However, it didn't stop me from trying to look as cute as possible whenever I was someplace where I either knew or suspected or could imagine him being.

Which was what happened over a magical Fourth of July weekend at a rented cabin at Grande Lake. There were twelve of us, not coupled, per se, but an even enough split for that kind of thing (if push came to shove, a grouping of three could be formed). It was a fun time, the weather perfect, bonfires, swimming, sunbathing on inflatable rafts we purchased at a three hundred percent markup at the local general store, Jared's shirtless torso (he had an eight-pack that was a tiny bit unsymmetrical...*grrr*). On the morning of the actual Fourth, a group of us went hiking. We stumbled across an abandoned mineshaft. Dares were made. Once Jared agreed to go inside, I made a show of bravery, venturing inside with him. The darkness caused vertigo, so much so that my trembling knees nearly buckled. Jared must've sensed my quiet panic, because he bumped into me (probably faked), and we wrapped our arms around one another, darkness so absolute not even our smiling teeth were visible.

That night, we played patriotic drinking games. I fell firmly into the category of *drunk* on *List those who'd signed the Declaration of Independence*. But I was a fun drunk, the good kind of sloppy, witty. Jared finally paid me attention. The rest of the world disappeared. I played up my bashfulness and said I'd been crushing on him for the better part of two years. He ate it up. He leaned close and said, "Then is this a dream come true?" He kissed me with a forceful tongue.

That night, we made love four times (for the Fourth, *obvi*). He held me while we slept.

The next morning, I woke up late, probably close to noon. Jared wasn't there. I climbed out of the cedar-logged bed and stumbled through the house. None of my friends were in the cabin. I made my way outside. The sun was like a serrated blade filleting my retinas. There were voices coming from the other side of the house. I recognized Jared's. Then I recognized Alexandra's (a girl I didn't love because she posed very real competition for Jared's affections).

I was about to turn the corner and mark my territory by greeting the man of my dreams with an erection-sprouting kiss, when Jared's words stopped me dead in my tracks: "That fire pit looks like Candace's asshole."

Alexandra laughed and said, "Gross."

"Seriously," Jared said. "It looked like a tire."

"You're so bad."

"She wanted it from behind but I kept staring at that frownie-brownie and dry heaving."

This broke me. So did his sharing it with Alexandra. Knowing that my anus was brown, and in turn, flawed, broke me.

I'm not sure if it was being called an FB that *actually* set in motion the following avalanche of bad life events—laid off from Sports Authority, fell out with my grouping of friends once Jared and Alexandra started dating, put on eleven pounds of Toll House cookie dough, my parents attempted a trial separation, Juan Pablo was on *The Bachelor*—but it couldn't all have been a coincidence. I'd sit in my apartment bored and lonely with a stomach ache from too many sweets. I'd tell myself I wasn't going to think about Jared's comments concerning my anus resembling a tire. I'd tell myself he was stupid and immature and was one stressful situation away from balding. This never helped. Eventually, I'd end up on my bed, legs over my head, handheld mirror illuminating my scarlet letter.

So that is my genesis story; I came into the field of anal beautification through humiliation for being an FB. I found out how to fix my own. I bleached it every other day for a month. Babe the pig had nothing on its healthy hue of desirable. The Internet said sixty percent of women had darkened bottoms. Online forums were full of embarrassed women, ashamed even. I realized I could kill two birds with one stone: make money so I didn't have to move back home with my *trial-separated* parents, and help out those in need.

I knew how to market. I knew how to work social media. And most importantly, I knew what it felt like to be disgusted by something you had never thought to be disgusted by before.

My business exploded.

The genius of my business model was my work being outcall. No self-respecting suburban mom would be caught dead stepping foot in Bridget's Bleaching. Not to mention, none of them had time between their children's play dates and gymnastics and mommy-and-me yoga classes. But a quick thirty-minute appointment while their little ones watched *Frozen*? Easy. I was discrete. I was gentle. I was able to make small talk with anyone while doing anything. I charged $125 a session. I averaged three appointments per day. Obama provided me insurance.

The other genius thing about my business model was knowing that everything tried to return to its natural state;

frownie-brownies strived for a darkened shade of shame, meaning everyone I saw was a repeat customer.

Fast-forward three years. Things were once again good: plenty of money, a smaller, closer-knit grouping of friends, Tinder dates that were at least a free meal. This all changed with a new client who lived in the condo section of Stapleton.

⋮

Sandy Casoli was the kind of skinny that made you want to cut your thighs. She appeared young, really young, like I almost asked to see her ID because I wasn't sure of the legality of bleaching a minor. I told her to give me a few minutes to set up, which I did in the master bedroom. I erected my massage table. I lit a few candles. I played some yoga music from my Bluetooth speakers. I told her to come in.

Sandy evidently knew she looked good, because she was naked when she walked into her bedroom. She nodded at the candles and told me it was a nice touch. She asked how I wanted her. I told her we'd start with her lying on her stomach.

She laughed.

I wasn't sure if she was nervous, or if I'd done something wrong.

"Kind of funny," she said. "How normal it is to walk into a bedroom and ask how the other person wants you."

I laughed. She climbed onto the table. I covered her bottom half with a thin sheet. I applied oil and started with a massage.

"It's bullshit, if you think about it," Sandy said. "I mean, why should we be the ones who are told what position to climb into? I mean, unless you're dealing with a guy who's packing some serious meat, there are all of two positions that actually have a chance of hitting the G, and there isn't a girl out there who likes doggy unless she's got self-esteem issues, am I right?"

I gave a polite laugh. I rubbed her lower back.

Sandy said, "Just the other night, my boyfriend insists on reverse cowgirl. He's all, *Come on baby, that shit's so hot.* I know it's pointless because his dick's all of six inches. I do it anyway. It's basically me just sitting there not moving because the smallest of up-and-downs causes his pecker to slip right out while he stares at my asshole."

People tended not to speak all that much while I performed my duty. On some level, they wanted the whole thing over with, never to have happened, and the sharing of any sort of banter made that a more difficult feat. Obviously, this wasn't the case with Sandy. I'd removed the sheet from her legs, continuing my massage, but also signifying it was nearing time for her to squat and spread. I paused when I reached her feet, which were absolutely enormous. I would've rather bleached a thousand homeless men than touched them. Luckily, I didn't have to, Sandy's next comment causing my limbs to numb.

"You know what he says to me? After I agree to sit on him and turn around so he can pretend he's in a porn? He says, "Jesus babe, your dirthole looks like a tire." Can you believe it? What a fucking dick, right?"

It was in that moment when I glanced over to Sandy's vanity. I saw a tacky heart-framed picture of her in some hideous silver dress standing next to an aged and balding Jared.

"Yet here I am about to have you give it a good scrubbing. Can't say us girls are winning much of anything, huh?"

I bleached Sandy, throwing in two strips of wax for free. I advised her to stay away from anything spicy for forty-eight hours. She told me I was the best and left me a twenty-dollar tip.

I was livid for the better part of a week. I couldn't stop thinking about Jared being the most hateful man alive, nothing but a misogynistic prick using his charm and stunning looks to shatter women's self-esteems through verbal degradation of their anuses. I reactivated my Facebook account, cyber-stalking him for hours a day. Judging from his pictures, he'd been dating Sandy for close to a year. They seemed serious, even posting a picture of them drunk at a Broncos game three days after I'd transformed her into a pinky-winkie. I kept thinking about what Sandy had said regarding men telling women what position to contort into. I thought about women doing whatever they had to in order to please men. I thought about my natural FB, and hated myself for giving myself a bleaching while cruising through Jared's profile pics. I replayed that fateful Fourth of July weekend when I overheard the man I thought I loved compare my asshole to a tire.

I said earlier there was no shame in being either a pinky-winkie or frownie-brownie. This is obviously a fallacy. There is great shame in being an FB; my own experience proves this. But there *shouldn't* be. There shouldn't. Contrary to prevailing wisdom, the darkened hue of one's anus has nothing to do with feces. You aren't *unclean* if you're rocking a little mulatto down there. Your concentration of blood cells simply takes on a darkened shade. But that doesn't matter. Not to men like Jared who gather all of their views about women from pornography. Not to women like Sandy and all of my other clients and not to myself who place these men on pedestals, so eager to overlook their physical, emotional, and spiritual flaws in order to achieve some fairy tale ideal of love, and in turn, to feel okay about ourselves, valid, worthy. It's bullshit. Bullshit I wasn't going to take anymore. My anus was root canal raw from my week of constant bleaching. I couldn't stop looking at Jared's pictures. I realized I wasn't *helping* women by giving them visas into the land of pinky-winkies; I was perpetuating the cycle of subjugation. I looked at Jared's most recent post about an open house he was hosting the following afternoon. I closed my computer, smiling, so careful waddling over to my bed.

I showed up the following afternoon to a Tudor near City Park. Jared's stupid face was plastered on a "For Sale" sign with orange balloons tied to its side. He'd tried to make the house presentable. There was a fresh coat of paint and some new shrubbery, but you could still tell it was the type of place with black mold growing behind every slab of sheetrock. I'd purchased an inflatable doughnut at Walgreens for my steak out. I'd also re-downloaded the Facebook app, which I combed through, my favorite pictures of Jared from three years before. It was strange to vacillate between lust and hatred and longing and disgust, but maybe not so strange, emotions of bodily amplification all the same.

After what appeared to be an unsuccessful three-hour open house, the lights cut, and Jared walked out of the front door. He looked kind of depressed. I fought the urge to rush to his side and tell him to keep his head up, the house would sell, he'd eventually move on from starter homes in sections of Denver that had to, at some point, gentrify. He clipped the balloons from his sign and let them fly away. I'm not much of an environmentalist, but this was a dick move, the blatant disregard for anyone but himself steeling my resolve for revenge.

I trailed his dated Lexus SUV. He stopped at a liquor store and then at Chick-Fil-A. I was invisible. We headed away from downtown, which meant he'd probably sold his condo, realizing he was past the stage of life when the *down-for-anything* persona was an asset. He drove to Stapleton. I cursed because he was probably headed to Sandy's. But he turned down a different street and then slowed and a garage door opened to a home that looked too big for a single man. When the garage door closed, I thought about it being sad inside of that house with its new appliances and unused rooms.

I sat there for longer than I needed to. Darkness came. I looked at one of Jared's pics from the Fourth of July weekend at Grande Lake. I was pretty sure my arm could be seen in the bottom left corner.

⋮

Being in the field of beautification (anal or otherwise), I had access to wholesale products. More importantly, I had access to certain chemicals used in various age-and-gravity defying concoctions. The night of my steak out, I went home and ordered three grams of Dihydroxyacetone (the darkening agent in self-tanner).

It arrived the next day in a rather sketchy looking package with a handwritten return address. The chalky white powder was in a clear plastic bottle, not unlike a film canister. I couldn't stop laughing, imaging Jared wiping his ass, the powder already spread across the entire roll, each attempt at cleanliness a damning smear of murk. I drove to Target to purchase a remote-controlled car, which was crucial for my breaking and entering. I was too giddy to sleep. I bleached myself while watching reruns of *Gilmore Girls*.

The next morning, I woke up early. I drove to Stapleton. It was still dark out when I crept to Jared's garage. I knelt down by a shrub and put the new remote-controlled monster truck a few feet from the door. I walked back to my car across the street. About an hour later the garage door opened, and out came Jared's tired-looking Lexus. He peeled out of the driveway.

Perfect.

I leaned toward my open window and drove the football-sized monster truck out of the shrubbery and onto the driveway and then through the closing garage door. The car tripped the safety sensor, and up went the door. Sometimes life was that easy.

I scurried from the car, realizing the hunched sprinting probably drew a bit of attention, so I righted my posture and acted like I'd been there before. I walked through the backdoor. His house was like I thought it would be—nice with nice things, but nice things purchased at the same moment on the same Pottery Barn credit card, sterile, unlived in, lonely—and I couldn't help but thinking about his home needing a woman's touch, a softening, a warming, something that made the house more than a desperate bargaining chip for some unlucky pinky-winkie who would someday be its prisoner. It took everything in my power not to refold his dishtowel jammed into the over handle.

His upstairs was more depressing with its tells of bachelorhood: a *Maxim* magazine (what boy over thirteen read those?), a trendy IPA on his nightstand, the slacks he'd worn at his open house two days prior—which he'd looked really good in—crumpled on the floor. I made my way to the bathroom. The white tile was littered with dead soldiers. His mirror was speckled with the insides of pimples. There was no soap on the sink. The towels gave off a steady belch of mold.

I got to work, unrolling the entire roll of TP on the floor. I made a snake, which dipped into the tub. I slipped on latex gloves, and then proceeded to sprinkle the Dihydroxyacetone onto the paper, using a makeup brush I'd brought with to spread the grains out evenly. I was careful to wipe my perspiring brow with my shoulders. The rolling back up of the toilet paper proved the most difficult phase of Operation Frownie-brownie, but Jared was a guy, and what guy even glanced away from Angry Birds while taking a shit, let alone studied the TP dispenser?

I finished my task.

It was time for my exit.

But something felt wildly anticlimactic about the whole thing. I mean, I knew the plan was stupid; Jared would probably never even glance at his asshole (especially not during the few weeks it would be remarkably tanned), but I'd felt good about *knowing* he was one of us who he bashed, if even for a month. Yet I felt like I hadn't done a thing. I wouldn't be there; I wouldn't be the one who got to shame him, saying there was a striking resemblance between his anus and a tire. But what if there was?

I sat down on the edge of his bed. The mattress was nice, probably memory foam. I was now gripped by a new plan, this one so much better, this one with actual teeth, this one capable of causing an equivalent amount of damage to his psyche as he'd caused me, this one involving me, a chance encounter, me looking too good to resist—*no, that wouldn't work, not with the memory of when I was a repulsive frownie-brownie*—so I'd send him a *sext*, something suggestive (both sexually and about how I now rocked pink), then quickly reply with fake horror, saying I'd sent it to the wrong number, please erase, blah, blah, blah. If my three years on Tinder had taught me anything, it was that the quickest way to a man's heart was through the mentioning of my work, which is to say my asshole, men never developing past Freud's anal stage. Jared would be intrigued. He wouldn't be able to resist. It'd take a single date for me to be back on this very same bed, for me to maneuver myself so I had a clear view of his horrible black hole.

I got off his bed (I'd evidently been a little tired and had lain down on his pillow, his aroma like a déjà vu of shame and Mr. Right and faking orgasms). My exit from his garage was better than my entrance; in fact, it felt natural walking down the driveway with a toy truck in my hand in a neighborhood I'd lately started to want to inhabit.

I bleached five anuses that day and three the next. By my eighth one, I experienced something I'd never before felt while doing my job: repulsion. I told myself this disgust was directed at the particular state of my last client's *derrière* (*tres* rough shape), but I knew that wasn't one hundred percent true. I couldn't help but judge this woman. She was probably forty, attractive in the way 7's age into being. She'd evidently never heard of a Brazilian. I charged her for the waxing. Instead of being gentle, I pulled the strips at an angle, almost like I was trying to irritate her skin as much as possible. Why? Because she wasn't trying. Or rather, she *was* trying, as in at this very moment, but it was too little too late. One doesn't wake up in a six-hundred-thousand-dollar home with two kids and a moderately impressive warrior pose and say to herself, *Gee, I think I'm going to make my anus less disgusting*. Not unless she was nudged in that direction. That nudge could've come from her husband or from her *suspicion* of her husband or maybe even from the sole stay-at-home dad mopping up at the community pool. But it'd come, and it'd come recently. I wanted to ask her why she was afforded *the dream* before being made aware of her FB? Why did she get to go through her twenties drunk and carefree and then her thirties with the white girl stressors of preschool selections and whether or not to eat glutton? Why hadn't I? Why couldn't I have been Sandy, meeting Jared three years later, his comments about the old tire still dickish, but not soul-shattering? Why had I let it consume me, define me, dictate my profession, cloud my view of every man I met, make me the one to suggest the teenage position of a sixty-nine because I was so eager for whatever guy to know I was a pinky-winkie?

I struggled to make my last client's wrinkles taut in order to get an even bleaching. For some reason, I thought of my own nudge—and honestly, I saw it that way for a split second, a nudge toward being better—and maybe it'd been my own insecurities that had caused it to take over my life? Maybe, just maybe, in a roundabout way, Jared's mean comments had helped me? And maybe this whole thing—my obsession and profession and bleaching Sandy and the dihydroxyacetone and my eventual reunion with Jared—was some trick the universe was so found of playing, fate and perseverance, the sad part of every romantic comedy before eternal happiness.

I sent Jared a staged pic of me getting out of the tub (POV left hand, floor-up), everything glistening. I sent over a text shortly afterward in all caps: OMG SO EMBARRASSING. THAT WAS SUPPOSED TO GO TO SOMEONE ELSE;)

My hands shook as I sat on the toilet, waiting. They started to shake even more when a minute stretched into five and then into thirty and I could hardly breathe when an hour had gone by and Jared still hadn't replied. I rushed to my computer and opened up Facebook. He hadn't advertised any open houses or anything that may be taking up his time. I checked Sandy's profile for any signs of them being together, but there was nothing. I refreshed my screen every five seconds. I willed my phone to ring. I checked and rechecked my photo, straining to see if I'd missed a spot, a microscopic smudge of dark, a strengthening of his repulsion. I sat like that all night, cold and shivering at my computer wrapped in a towel. My phone stayed silent; Jared's Facebook went un-updated.

⋮

The messages started appearing the next morning: *Hang in there, buddy; We're all praying for you; If anyone can make it through something like this, it's you, man; We love you so much.*

Finally, his mother posted a declarative message: *On Wednesday evening, Jared experienced three grand mal seizures as the result of a severe allergic reaction. He was rushed to St. Luke's Presbyterian. He went into anaphylactic shock, and slipped into a coma. The doctors are optimistic he will make his way through this ordeal. Please pray for our amazing son. Flowers can be sent to room 544, but at this time, we ask for privacy.*

I started to cry.

I'd nearly killed him.

I was a wreck. That day was a blur of crying and Facebook and reaching out to the friends from my *yo-pro* days that had abandoned me. I even texted Alexandra, the girl Jared had made fun of me with and later dated. I needed details. Did the doctors know what had caused the allergic reaction? Was he getting better? Was he going to die?

Nobody knew anything.

I cancelled all of my appointments.

I researched allergic reactions to dihydroxyacetone, and yes, there were plenty, some of them deathly serious. I grew terrified—the shakes that had never really gone away were back like a life-threatening case of DT's—when I thought about somebody having seen me creep in and out of his house. Maybe one of the Stapleton moms rose early to catch a 5:30 CrossFit class and noticed a woman sneaking into his open garage? Maybe they had cameras on all of the lampposts to thwart crime or people with dark skin from walking down their sidewalks? And then I thought about fingerprints. And then I thought about the photo I'd sent him. And then I thought about the record of my dihydroxyacetone purchase. And then I thought about digital footprints, the cyber stalking, the Google search for allergic reactions.

I smashed my laptop.

I stuck the pieces into the microwave because I'd seen a character do that in a show about hackers.

I allowed myself to check Facebook on my phone because that could be explained.

I cancelled my appointments the following day.

I quit eating.

I bleached.

I read updates from his mother and sister: Jared was still in a coma; the doctors had figured out what had caused the allergic reaction; CT's showed great brain activity; more prayers were needed.

I wasn't sure if it was guilt or fear or the lack of sleep, but I came dangerously close to turning myself in. This seemed like the only way out of the shakes and vomiting and incessant checking of updates. I needed to tell the police it'd been a small prank gone horribly awry. Hopefully I'd be confessing my sins to a woman cop, a frownie-brownie who knew it, one who had been made to feel disgusting by a man over the course of her life. She'd understand it was a small act of vengeance, a one-in-a-million chance of ending up like this. She'd tell me it wasn't my fault. She'd tell me to keep my mouth shut. She'd tell me nobody deserved to die, but a man who belittled and shamed about what God had so freely gifted us, deserved a few weeks of a darkened anus, which was all I'd been trying to do.

After a week, I realized I wasn't going to confess. My door had yet to be knocked on; the police weren't coming. I had to get on with my life. I had to return to work. I had to act like everything was good. So I did. I rescheduled all of the sessions I'd canceled. I set up my massage table and dimmed lights and lit candles and tried to block out *Dora the Explorer* from family rooms as I bleached assholes. Sometimes I would cry. Sometimes I was certain unmarked sedans were trailing me. Sometimes I understood I could get through life with this secret, and it wouldn't be easy, wouldn't be fun, but I could do it, *was* doing it, *had* to do it. It would always be there. It would be in every client and every self-bleaching and every thirty-year-old male who wore ironic trucker hats and in every Lifetime movie I watched and every nightmare that didn't end when I awoke. It would be a stain on my psyche, my soul, but it would lessen, the hue of it lightening until it provoked a catch in my breathing instead of a sob.

Two weeks went by.

Jared was still in a coma.

The posts on his Facebook wall became less frequent.

I received an online booking from Sandy Casoli. I was about to reject the request when I realized this could actually be a good thing. She was a talker, and it wouldn't take much to get her to open up. I could get precious intel on any possible police involvement. Thirty minutes with her would do great things to alleviate my free-floating anxiety about a life spent in prison.

That Friday, I showed up to her condo. She greeted me less enthusiastically than she had the first time. She still looked amazing, like she was fifteen years old, but her eyes were sunken from tears and lack of sleep. I set up my table. She disrobed before I had my candles lit. She lay on her stomach. I applied oil. I asked her how everything was going.

"Shitty."

"Yeah?"

I waited for her to elaborate, but she didn't. I rubbed her shoulders. I said, "More disagreements with the boyfriend?"

"Why would you say that?"

"I...it's just last time I was here, you seemed a little upset with him."

Sandy raised her head, glaring at me. I smiled my best smile. She let her head fall back to the table with a soft thud.

"Sorry," she said. "Stressed like a motherfucker. And sick of answering questions about him."

"Oh."

"He's in the hospital," Sandy said.

"Oh my God, is he okay?"

"Yeah. No. I don't know. It's so fucked up. He had some allergic reaction and has been in a coma for like two weeks. So fucking sad."

I didn't have to act; my empathy came organically. I said things about that being horrible and so scary and I sniffled a real sniffle, the tears coming.

"It's like you never know, you know?"

"Totally," I said.

"One day I'm complaining about him to you, the next he's having a seizure as we're watching *Varsity Vamps*. Boom. Snap of the fingers."

"But he'll get better?"

"After seventy-two hours, the chances of him coming out drop to less than ten percent."

"I'm so sorry. Is there...anything I can do?"

Again with the head raise and glare. I had to keep my goddamn mouth shut and tears in check. I gave a pouty nod. Sandy relaxed.

She said, "You can tell me there's a point to any of this."

"Any of *this*?"

"What we're doing right here."

"The bleaching?"

"Sure."

"Umm...I guess so your bottom is more appealing to a larger cross-section of America?"

"You hear how ridiculous that sounds?" Sandy laughed a depressed laugh. "My boyfriend is going to die, and I'm having my shitter bleached. It's like the perfect fucking example of how pointless everything is. How we worry about shit that doesn't matter. Because none of it matters. Nothing."

I'd moved on to her gigantic feet.

"I love him, I really do," Sandy said.

"I know."

"I may not have always shown it, but I did. As much as I'm capable of. I sure as fuck didn't poison him."

My hands gave an involuntary clench.

"Ouch. Easy on the bunion," Sandy said.

"Poison?"

"Yeah. That's pretty much what the detectives were grilling me about. I mean, I have enough going on, like trying to keep all my shit together and be there for him and his family, and they're asking me about disagreements and fights and whatnot."

"I'm sorry," I said. "You guys seemed happy."

Sandy turned yet again, this time using her elbow for purchase. She exuded nothing but distrust. And why wouldn't she? I was being an idiot, saying too much, my latest comment pretty much an admission to cyber stalking the man I'd loved and then put into a coma.

"I'm sorry," Sandy said, "but how the hell would *you* know?"

"From how you talked about him," I said.

"Complained that he was a dick?"

"But in a fun way. Like you loved him so much *despite* his comments."

Sandy stared. I smiled, which felt like too much, so I slipped my mouth into a frown.

"Why are you sweating so badly?" she asked.

"Low blood sugar."

Sandy sat up. She was skinny enough that none of her stomach spilled over on itself.

"Here's what I don't understand," Sandy said. "Why is it you're pretending you have no idea who Jared is?"

A series of antidepressant withdrawal eclectic shocks sizzled through my brain. My head started to shake, my voice evidently on sabbatical.

"Yeah. I know you know him. He told me about you. Told me the whole story after I'd complained about wanting a pinker shitter. Said he'd been with some girl with the dirtiest asshole he'd ever seen. He said he'd called it a tire. He said you'd started your own bleaching service."

I wasn't sure if I was going to cry or scream or start throwing punches.

"Figured I'd look you up, check up on the former competition, two birds one stone."

"I...I..."

"Still love him? Obviously."

"No. I didn't know if it was professional—"

"To bleach the asshole of the woman the guy you're obviously still in love with is banging? Yeah, I don't know the correct protocol on that one. But being like this? All weepy and shaky while you're asking thinly veiled questions? That's probably not the best play."

"I'm sorry. I didn't know…I feel bad for you."

"Don't," Sandy said. She stood. The skin over her hips had the thinnest of stretchmarks, but almost like they'd formed from a rapid constriction rather than expansion.

She walked to her vanity. She looked at the framed picture of her and Jared. She pulled out a stack of twenties and then turned, meeting my eyes, no smile, a challenge.

"I don't really trust you," Sandy said. "Especially your comment about us *looking* happy." She dropped the money on my massage table. She said, "That comment is some creepy-ass shit."

⋮

Things went from bad to worse rather quickly after that appointment. Any ten-minute fitful bursts of sleep I'd been able to steal vanished. My mind was a thousand hypothetical scenarios, each and every one a Vine clip of my future, which, more often than not, resulted in me wearing orange behind bars. Every second was a battle of fear and logic, rationalizations versus possibilities. I quit eating. I kept my appointments, but dropped the massages from my repertoire. I deleted Facebook and reinstalled it three times on my phone. Jared was still in Neverland. I waited for Sandy to tell the police I'd known Jared, had been hurt by him, had been *devastated* by him, and the timing of me coming into her life was perfect with his allergic reaction, the catalyzing agents sent straight to my apartment. And there was the tasteful photo I'd sent Jared, which was probably still on his phone.

After another three days of zero calories and a total of two hours of sleep, the knocking on my door finally arrived. I was in the bathroom bleaching. The shower ran, but I heard the pounding, an angry wrapping of knuckles and then maybe the meaty part of a fist. I thought about playing deaf, just hiding, praying there was no warrant, thus no breaking down of my door. The knocking kept up. I'd have to face them sooner or later; better to get it over with. I'd play innocent and maybe I could make something up about the tanning agent being part of my régime, like maybe I used it as a reverse White Out if I over-bleached a certain anus. The police would ask about the picture I'd sent him and I could say we'd been a thing, back a few years ago and then more recently, maybe he'd been an off-the-books client, but once clothes were shed, bygones were bygones, old flames ignited, that kind of thing.

I put a towel around my chest and waddled to the door. I peered through the peephole, which was nothing but blurry distortion. I opened the door.

Sandy stood there looking like a hot mess, so much of her hair not in its pony.

"Sandy?"

"Were you fucking him?"

"What?"

She thrust an iPhone in my face. I looked at the bottom curve of my left butt cheek with a hint of my PW.

"That was a mistake," I said. "I meant to send it to this other guy, *Jack*. Jared and Jack are obviously right next to one another in my contacts. I was so embarrassed."

Sandy didn't respond. She pushed her way through the door. She looked around my apartment, running her hand through her hair, pressing against her temples.

"How long?" she said.

"Sandy, please, let's calm down and talk about—"

"How long?" she yelled.

"It was a mistake."

"Don't play me like I'm some thirteen-year-old bitch who has no idea how this world works. Nobody *sexts* by accident. Nobody flashes her beav in a skirt by accident. Women know exactly how to yield the body. So don't play the *Bambi* card with me."

While my head was shaking *no*, my mind assessed the situation, trying to determine the actual threat Sandy posed, if it was immediate or if it started once she left the room and dialed *911*.

"Why don't you put on your big girl panties and be straight with me? Can you do that? Are you *capable* of that?"

She wasn't near any of my knives. I was bigger than her, had her by at least five pounds (probably closer to fifteen).

"Just be real with me, okay? Like I'm spending every second of my day sitting by the bed of some motherfucker who may have been pounding your dirty ass the whole time. Do you know what that's like? No. Of course you don't. But to be tied to a man you all of a sudden can't trust? It's...please tell me the truth."

She'd lost some steam. Her anger had already turned inward. She wasn't going to hurt me, at least not physically. All she wanted to know was if the man she was sentenced to be a martyr for had been faithful. I could give her this. I could give her this peace of mind, which she wouldn't thank me for, but it would save her life. It'd allow her the strength to persevere. It'd allow her to play the role of choice for every American: a sole heroine all strung up on that cross with so many people weeping at her feet.

But for some reason I didn't want to give her this peace of mind. I wanted to punish her for doing too little too late. For being able to make it into her thirties without knowing she'd never outrun her disgusting asshole. For being a frownie-brownie, but that not mattering to Jared.

I said, "Jared always told me how big your feet were, but I simply had to see it for myself."

Sandy's entire face crumbled. I felt like Jared. I felt like Alexandra who'd stolen him by being an accomplice in my FB bashing. I felt like every man and woman ever who used physical traits to wield power over others.

"The thing I can't believe is that your feet are actually *bigger* than he'd always told me."

Sandy cried. She was too broken to scream or hit. She walked out of my apartment. I locked the door. I knew she'd want to wash her hands of Jared and his coma and the detectives, which would mean she would tell them about me (if she hadn't already). I knew I had to act quickly. Only one of us would be able to make it out unscathed, because that was the way the world worked, inverse relationships, ups and downs, winners and losers, pinky-winkies and frownie-brownies.

I called the police. I said I needed to speak to a detective. I was transferred to a woman. I gave her my name. I told her I had reason to suspect foul play, which resulted in my lover being in a coma. I told her the whole story, or *a* story, one that could be seen as a version of truth: the girlfriend of my lover found out about our affair; she hired me to bleach her anus; during our first session, she'd complained about how her boyfriend had always made her feel horrible about the darkened hue of her anus, and she'd asked about playing a practical joke on him, *did I know any way to make his ass dark as night?*; I'd jokingly suggested self-tanner applied to his toilet paper; the crazy girlfriend must've employed this method, to which my lover had evidently had a severe allergic reaction to and was now in an everlasting sleep.

The detective hung on my every word. She mentioned having liked Sandy for the crime all along.

⋮

That night, I drove to St. Luke's Presbyterian. I wore yoga gear, understated yet leaving nothing to the imagination. I took the elevator to the fifth floor. I walked to room 544. The hallway was dark with the subdued sounds of machines beeping and floor buffers and nurses conversing about their misbehaved children. Jared's room was empty. He lay there in a white gown with small baby blue diamonds. Tubes leaked from his mouth. A wall of machines cast his face in a golden aura. I stood by the side of his bed. I touched his limp hand. I liked the way our fingers fit together. I told him I was finally there. I apologized it'd taken so long for me to come see him, but certain things had to be taken care of first. I told him I liked the white and blue on him; it reminded me of the synthetic polo he'd worn the first time I'd seen him so many years before. I told him I was jealous of all the sleep he was getting. I was pretty sure he laughed, or at least his eyelids fluttered. I told him I was going to right all of my wrongs. He seemed to think this was a nice gesture. I walked to the end of the bed. His legs were heavy to lift, but I was able to get them up and over each of my shoulders. I told him I forgave him for how he'd treated me at the cabin in Grande Lake. We were young then, I said. So young. Stupid. We didn't understand the body, especially taboo things like anuses. I was gentle moving his penis and catheter to the side. I giggled. I told him it made more sense now, his projections of anal hue discrimination, what with him having the darkest frownie-brownie I'd ever seen. We'll get that cleaned up in a jiffy, I said. It's nothing to be ashamed about. Contrary to popular belief, the color of one's bottom has nothing to do with feces stains, but is the result of age and genetics and diet and pigmentation. It's nothing to be embarrassed about, Jare-Bear, nothing at all. I brushed his asshole. This might sting a little bit, but it's worth it, believe me, baby, so very worth it. I told him it wasn't permanent, but not to worry, because I could do it once a month, maybe even twice a month if he felt extra insecure. Because we have nothing but time, honey. So much time. I'm not going anywhere.

I stared into his cavity.

The beeping of the machines was a heartbeat, a shared one, Jared's and mine.

I remembered the hike we'd all gone on in the mountains. I remembered the old mining shaft we'd uncovered. Alexandra had been too frightened to venture inside—*it's okay, hon, it's obvious she wasn't right for you, but we have to have those experiences, it's how we end up with our soul mates, don't you see?*—but I'd summoned a shred of courage, following Jared inside. The temperature had dropped enough to cause shivers. It'd been complete blackness. I'd searched for my phone for light, but Jared had stopped me. This had been our first purposeful touch, Jared's hands on mine, his hand lingering, the darkness making him brave, the two of us functioning through other senses, our fear bubbling over into an embrace and nervous giggles. I'd wanted to tell him to never let me go. But that's the funny thing about life; sometimes you're able to speak the words you'd failed to utter the first time. I told Jared I'd never leave his side. We embraced the darkness, finally realizing it gave us the cover to be our true selves, shy kisses in the cave and in room 544, dreams coming true, our bodies ceasing to exist with the absorption of all light.

⋮

I wish the story ended there. Needless to say, it didn't.

The cops came calling four days later. Within a fortnight, I was under arrest. I was charged with attempted murder. The silver lining is that Jared came out of his coma while I was awaiting my trial. I plead down to Breaking and

Entering and Attempted Man Slaughter, three years with the carrot of good behavior shaving off a few months.

Prison isn't bad.

I mean, it's horrible, but it's not like in the movies. My cellie, Olga, is the biggest Russian woman on the yard. In exchange for bleaching her into a proud pinky-winkie, she keeps me safe. In fact, I have a business, which, if I do say so myself, is flourishing. With nothing but time and girl-on-girl cunnilingus, extra concern is paid to the colors of our anuses. I'm paid in choice hard goods. I hand these over to Olga, who divvies them out for favors and power.

I, for one, have quit bleaching, partially because the bleach I use is straight from the industrial cleaning supplies we siphon off, but mostly because I've learned that having a dark asshole is nothing to be ashamed of. This lesson took me a while to fully grasp—not to mention my freedom—but it's important, nevertheless. I mean, like fuck it: I'm a frownie-brownie, so deal.

But maybe that isn't even the whole truth.

Because every night as I'm drifting off to sleep amidst the snores of Olga and the screams of the angry and the moans of those lucky enough to be bunked with lovers, I think about that mine shaft in the mountains. I remember Jared holding me. I remember the blackness. And I think about life being funny, how it takes patience to fully comprehend its magical design. I think about my time in prison being a small layover to the happily-ever-after I'll share with Jared. The world wouldn't make us both frownie-brownies for no reason. Birds of a feather...

We the Cucks

I

We are the men wearing windbreakers with our company's insignia stitched across the left breast, those anonymous sad sacks standing at the periphery of the playground as our two-point-five play with other too-aggressive children, our hands full with a venti Starbucks, two helmets, a Strider, a three-speed, and a ringing phone, our wives frantic on the other end about the garbage that was not taken out a half hour before.

You'd be able to recognize us from our smiles: a thousand shades of *this is everything I've ever wanted and I love my life and children and wife and my job and the fact that a thirty-five waist would be embarrassed to say it was able to contain our newfound guts*, all of us smiling, laughing (usually without actual sound), all of us armed with wipes and Band-Aids and organic fruit squeezers, all of us thinking our best defense is a flashing of teeth, which we are planning on whitening someday soon.

We're regulars at Noodles and Panera. We play fantasy football. We have unused gym memberships. Some of us golf with friends, but we pay for this four-hour vacation from Saturdays around the house with *honey-do* lists, or worse, a cataloging of defects hurled at us with such ease that it makes us wonder if our wives actually *do* write these shortcomings down for just these occasions. We don't know when we started tucking in our shirts. We masturbate in our studies and sometimes in the handicapped bathroom at work. We pretend to care about throw pillows and accent walls, and then hold our tongues when our visions of Perfect Home clash with those of our significant others. Our hairlines are weather-beaten coasts. The last concert we attended was *Yo Gabba Gabba On Ice.* We live by antiquated rules of inference: I love my family; I need to provide for my family; therefore, I love providing for my family.

We know things will someday even out; our wants will bust through the WWI trenches of the desires of our children and wives. We tell ourselves we are strong. We are loving. We are what a man should be in the twenty-first century. And someday soon, our sacrifices will be noticed, and if not appreciated, at least jotted down underneath that never-ending list of failures and shortcomings.

II

It's a Friday afternoon and we all climb inside of our practical modes of transportation—Camrys and Foresters—and we put on a recently downloaded *Girl Talk* album (the artsy intern at the office was listening to it in her cubicle and we'd stopped by, said something about the music being catchy, us just trying to get a smile, us saying the music was *rad*, the interns laughing, embarrassed for us and our entire age bracket), and we like the fact we recognize some of the sampled songs from our own youth, times we remember as being nothing but red plastic cups and random insertions of our penises (were they bigger back then?), and we're in a pretty good mood, the sun low in the sky, the work week over with, forty-eight hours of doing whatever we want an obtainable horizon. We fight off the absurdity of this thought with affirmations: the kids will already have bathed; they will be happy to see us; our wives will have grilled steaks; the table will be set; they will greet us at the door. But it won't be like a '50s replica of domestication. No, it will be better because *we* are better than our fathers. We will help with the dishes. We will read our children stories. We will tell our wives to kick up their feet. And we know after our fifth *Olivia* book, we will look up from our children's beds. Our wives will be standing in the doorway. We will know they are thinking about us being amazing fathers, loving like they only dreamed of having for themselves, and how they are lucky to have us, and then a smile—sly, one we haven't seen since college, one promising not only copulation, but a little anal play (a finger, for we are not greedy)—and we will feel a crushing sense of gratitude, both toward our family and our amazing wives, but also toward every choice we've ever made, every pair of slacks we've paid to have hemmed, every recital sat through and trip to Vegas turned down, everything all of a sudden worth it, just like we knew it would be.

We turn into our driveways. We get out of the car with more pep than we've had since our junior varsity careers ended twenty years before. We're struck by the idea of being stealth; we will sneak in, which will grant us the sublime sight of our family in their element, while also providing a fun startling of *Here's Daddy!* We creak open our front doors. We are careful, stepping over scooters that our children promised to keep in the garage. We strain our ears for the melodic chorus of our beautiful family. We can't hear them. They must be in the kitchen. We creep across the flooring that singlehandedly added seven thousand dollars of interest to our mortgages. The kitchen is empty. There's no dinner. There's no toddler in her highchair. There's no smells of steak or even of Hamburger Helper hotdish.

Hmm.

We think we hear something above us.

We angle our heads as if they're antennas.

Yes, there it is, movement from the second floor.

The smile is back on our faces. We're light in our Kenneth Cole slip-ons. We ascend the steps. We try to make out our children's laughter. We think we can hear our wives' gentle corrections of behavior: *yes, yes, right there.*

They must be building something.

It's probably a surprise for us, because why else would they all be inside the closed master bedroom?

We compose ourselves; we strive for an unsuspecting facial expression.

We open the door.

We see anonymous men so much like ourselves, men who may have been on the sidelines of our children's soccer games, men who, moments before, were invisible with their card-carrying smile of Sexless Defeated Family Man. We see our wives' bodies contorted in positions we'd been told *isn't going to happen* fifteen years prior. We don't know what to do. We don't know if this is real. We think about screaming and we think about crying and we think about rushing over to our West

Elm kings and ripping this stranger off of our wives, our fists used for something other than kneading Play-Doh.

But we don't do anything.

Or rather, we do, and that something is to sneak back out of the room. We're so careful to set the handle without making an audible *click*. We are ghosts traveling down our staircases. We try in vain not to look at the pictures (all hung in a perfect diagonal line, which wasn't easy, mind you), but we do. We see our children who don't deserve a shattered home. We see our wedding photos, our cake-smeared faces, our naivety that we were about to start the best times of our lives. We walk back outside. We climb into our cars. We know the start of our engines won't break the sound barrier of the ruckus we'd just witnessed. We put our cars in reverse. *Girl Talk* still plays. Its ADHD beats sound confusing and too loud. We drive down the street. We go the speed limit. We see one of our friends. He drives his tasteful matte black Outback (he's a bit of a rebel). We give a two-finger wave from our steering wheels. Our friends do the same. But there's something different with him, and maybe with ourselves, because he cranes his neck as we pass by, just as we're doing, unsure what the hell is sticking out from the side of his head.

III

We all have that trippy *I lost my shit after seeing the love of my life fornicating like an Eastern Block porn star and now I'm staring in a mirror seeing things that can't possibly be there* moment. Some of us do this in our cars. Some of us find gas station bathrooms. Some of us use storefronts to restaurants we'd frequented as a happy family.

We stare at ourselves, like really study our faces, our heads, our tear-rimmed eyes, and our antlers.

Yes, antlers.

They come in all shapes and sizes, from a fawn's fuzz covered toothpicks to NBA center-sized moose racks. Most of ours are diamond-hard, sharpened, and nearly impossible to fit through our lowered Camry ceilings. We touch them. We pull. We twist. We sneak into Home Depot (okay, Lowe's, but same diff) to purchase handheld hacksaws. We cut and we rip and we blink away blood and tears and then stare back in the mirror, only to see our antlers in full, mating glory.

This is all within an hour of seeing what we saw. We stop what we are doing, telling ourselves to breathe, to calm down, to be rational about the situation. It's then we realize nobody is looking at us. Nobody seems to notice our antlers. But that's not completely true, because all of us have that first conversation, us in the checkout lines at Lowe's or in a public restroom at a turnoff three miles from our homes, us seeing another dad bod type with twists of bone rocking out from above his ears, us stopping, staring—*Can you? Can you? What the...? Are they real? Feels real*—and it doesn't take long for us to see our own kind, the normally invisible half of society with our Dr. Scholl's inserts and phones with our Redtube apps four screens away from the rest of the icons, for us to understand what has happened, all of our stories the same: *guttural* not even close to being a strong enough descriptor for the sounds escaping our wives' panting mouths.

IV

Some of us go to meetings. Cuckold Anonymous (CA) groups sprout up instantly (not to be confused with *Cocaine* Anonymous, which more than once proved to be bit uncomfortable for all involved parties in drafty church basements). We walk through rec center doors sideways so as to fit our racks. We space our metal folding chairs three feet apart for the same reason. We talk about the Moment of Reckoning (rules have to be set in place because a whole subgroup of us relish in these details, perversions of humiliation and emasculation evidently like dormant cancer among our demographic). We talk about how we're coping with our antlers. We talk about various strategies we've employed in efforts to free ourselves from our ailments. We talk about our families. We talk about sitting at dinner while our sons pretend to eat their peas and our daughters drone on and on about how they were slighted during *Show-and-Tell* and while our wives sip merlot with a dignity we suspect is new, perhaps a learned habit from nooners with their lovers. Some of us cry. Some of us talk about betrayal. Some of us talk about not understanding *why.* Those of us who seem to be handling the whole thing a little better than others say it's okay, it's all part of His plan, everything happens for a reason, someday we all will be grateful to be recovering cucks (it's usually us well-adjusted, godly types who meet in the parking lot afterward for the "real" meeting, i.e., one where we swap the juicy details of the five W's of our humiliating devastation).

Most of us grow bored with the meetings.

We believe our problem lies not with our antlers, but with the fact we were the type of men to sprout horns in the first place. We actually start going to the gym. We download another *Girl Talk* album. Some of us buy Jettas. We shave in places we didn't know men could shave. We whiten our teeth. We smile when our wives notice, tell them it was just time to start taking care of ourselves. We meet up after work. We sit in booths with our antlers bashing into kitsch nailed to the wall, all of us in our new duds (everything slim fit for our new rocking bods), and we drink more than we should, but *should* is a tool of shame, and honestly, we have nothing to be ashamed about any longer. This is what we tell ourselves. "I tell you what," we say, "ever since walking in on Janice with that ball gag in her mouth, I have never felt better. I am finally free." We give sloppy cheers to this every time. And just as quickly, we go quiet, silent actually, each of us thinking about our own Janices with their own ball gags, and then about us, too old of men in Chili's trying to shut the place down, us desperate for attention and validation and a way to make it all stop hurting.

We turn to the flesh.

We give leniency on our rating scales and then we abandon the whole concept, telling ourselves it's sexist and degrading, us *really* knowing it's because we're scraping at a handful of ones and twos. We think we are evening the scales and we think we are living the dream and we think we are extending our youths and then we climax and then our antlers cause nerves to pinch and we are covered in sweat (we tell ourselves it's from our own bodies) and then we are left with the memories of our children's births and our starter homes and the moment our wives first slipped their hands into ours, how it felt different, soap stone statues fitting together with the grace of a snowflake.

Eventually, we find it easier to stay home.

We're not exactly sure why this is, but we have our unsaid suspicions: at home, nobody can see our antlers, and if it weren't for the nightly baths of Icy Hot on our cramping necks, we'd be able to forget ourselves. We return to domestication. We say we're saving money by getting coffee at home instead of Starbucks. We start knocking off items on our *honey-do* lists, often over-extending ourselves and our perceived abilities. We learn to keep heads down when we leave the house (part of this is practical so as to not bash into our doorjambs, but mostly it's to avoid the sight of other pathetic cucks). We fall into a rhythm, a routine, our smiles back, but a little less aggressive, a rarity to actually show off our new sparkling whites.

We think this is life.

We think this is everything we could possibly want.

We think about life before and how good we had it, how our silent resentments were nothing but ungratefulness, how we'd give anything to still view our wives' refusal for Missionary Monday to be about her feeling tired and bloated, or at worst, about us and our hairy guts (anything but her being worn out from an afternoon romp). We tell ourselves we would have been better. We would've given massages without getting erections. We would have napalmed the house with fresh flowers. We would've agreed to couple's retreats. We would never have complained about a Saturday afternoon spent visiting a handful of boutiques before a tapas dinner that left us starving. Yes, we are ruined with regret, with *only ifs*, with *I would've's*. Some of us come pretty damn close to prayer. And then one day these unsaid prayers are answered.

V

Cuck-No-More runs an aggressive marketing campaign, a print, radio, television, and Internet attack perfectly tailored to those of us in need of saving. Every time we click on a *stud destroys wife* clip, we are granted the gift of an impossible-to-minimize pop-up ad with a cartoon hubby with antlers, the caption reading *Got Antlers? Cuck-No-More can help*. We read the same ad in the back of *GQ, Wired,* and *Golf Digest*. When we are "just looking" on Craigslist's *casual encounters*, and come across *anybody will do*, and accidentally click the link...yup, lo and behold, the same cartoon antler-riddled schlep appears. Late night reruns of *Two and a Half Men*, ESPN radio, the bathrooms at low testosterone clinics...everywhere we turn, *Cuck-No-More*, a promise at salvation, at redemption, all of us setting our calendars for a webinar in a week's time where we are promised a cure for our despicable manifestations of not being good enough.

That following Wednesday, all of us with horns and antlers and in need of thousands of dollars' worth of chiropractic corrections sit at our computers. Most of us have lied to our wives, telling them we needed to stay late at the office. They complained, but then nodded, and we of course took this as them mentally scheduling a pool cleaning. We sit in our cubicles, the majority of a five-dollar foot-long cached at our sides. Our ties are inched downward. We feel stupid, but assure ourselves we aren't *that* big of suckers because we haven't handed over any money. We keep refreshing our screens. We shake with nerves. We need this to work.

Finally, our screens change. A figure live-streams into countless darkened insurance agencies. We can't tell who, or even *what*, this person is because he/she is shadowed-out, his/her voice robotized three octaves lower than humanly possible.

The darkened figure says, "You are all cucks. You are emasculated men, boys pretending to be grown up, your failures evident in your wives' indiscretions, and your subsequent racks."

We swallow a dry heave.

The voice tells the degradation-seekers amongst us to get our hands out of our pants.

"This isn't up for speculation or debate," the voice says. "It simply *is*. You, who equate the insertion of a phallus into a body that doesn't belong to you to your own self-worth, are between a rock and a hard place."

The voice pauses, laughing: "Or should I say a *cuck* and a hard place."

None of us finds this funny.

"You can either continue on with your lives full of antlers and crushing insecurities, or..."

We all turn up the volume on our company Dells.

"Or be given a chance to redo the entirety of time from the first moment you saw your wife to this very second."

Those of us who'd been slow to slip our hands out of our slacks finally do. We lean closer to our monitors. We pray this *Locked-Up* witness-protection informant is telling the truth.

"But I have to warn you," the voice says. "There is no guarantee that events will follow in the same manner. Your children may not be born. You may get T-boned by a semi the second you awake in your past. Iraq may actually develop weapons of mass destruction. The Internet may never be developed."

We pause on the voice's last scare tactic, our fingers hovering over our mice.

"It is not *your* past. You will simply be transported back to the exact moment you first saw your wife, and then life and time and chaos and fate will do what they may. The only recollection you will have of *this* life will be the faintest and most random sense of déjà vu, a small and silent hint of intuition. Do not tread lightly with this decision. Think about your families. Think about the abundance of gifts you've managed to accumulate. Know that all of these blessings could be stripped from you by clicking *yes* on the bottom of the screen."

Silly Robotic God, like we give a fuck.

The collective echo of our double-clicks on *yes* sounds like the cracking of the earth's core.

VI

We're the men others wish they were, or at least could be friends with. We're twenty-something's and we're ascending tax brackets and our stomachs are one crunch away from the unicorn-rare *eight pack*. We're on the fast track to the New American Dream, one where we work hard, but not really that hard, half our "workday" spent on computers in Internet cafés, our dotcom startups bound to hit, us destined to not only be rich but famous, the real cultural currency. We don't need to be doctors or lawyers or bankers like our fathers because there's a definite ceiling in those outdated professions, and we're all about new frontiers, exponential growth, this World Wide Web thing a can't-miss.

Not to mention we have the hottest piece of ass around at our sides.

We say *piece of ass* to save a little face, but really, it's so much more than that. This girl, she's everything. She's like a guy who loves football and extreme sports and can put down a pitcher in less than an hour, meaning she's all sorts of fun to hang out with. She's smart. She's sexy. And don't even get us started about how she is in the bedroom…okay, if you're going to twist our arms…let's just say more often than not, it's *us* who has to eventually throw in the towel, suggest we maybe watch an episode of *Real World San Francisco* just so we're able to walk the next morning.

We are going to take over the world.

We are going to do it in a fashion unlike any previous generation, one where we put a premium on fun, on individuality, on never outgrowing a relaxing joint split between our fiancées and ourselves. Yes, we've popped the question. Because our girls are perfect. They are the envy of every man and woman. They will always be down for whatever.

They are our best friends. We knew the moment they said *I would rather die than have children* that our search for a soul mate was complete.

Which makes what we're doing right now—B's D in the new intern at our dotcom startup—a little difficult to rationalize. We can, of course, because we're young and not married quite yet and we're men and it's pretty much in our DNA to sow as many seeds as possible, but there must be a little guilt there, because we think we hear the door to our lofts open. We peer over the tattooed clavicles riding us. We must be tripping because we think we see the door closing a centimeter at a time. We shake our heads. We keep up with our PG-13 indiscretions. But when we hear the unmistakable turn-over and eventual catch of our fiancées' Jeeps, we are struck with a weird sense of déjà vu, a memory that is probably a dream, us backing out of driveways, our worlds crumbled through the sight of our perfectly-aged wives riding some random dude, our necks aching from some unyielding weight, some horrible, computer glitch sounding music blasting away our eardrums.

We squeeze our eyes together.

Here comes the climax.

And with it, the weird, out-of-body experience fades, and our unabashed cocksureness returns—we are young; we will be rich and famous; we will get everything we want from life; our fiancées will never change; we will not be domesticated— and we laugh into the exposed brick of our lofts, thinking how ludicrous that vision had been, as if we'd ever be the types of guys to be cucked.

Well

I was just waiting for this Santa Claus-looking motherfucker to put his hand on my leg. I watched his stubby fingers grip the wheel, but there was no white in his knuckles and his country was fine and he drove and it was warm and my eyes were heavy.

I expected him to be like what's a pretty girl like you doing hitchhiking? Don't you know it's dangerous out there? Perverts and rapists and guys who want to do bad things to a little thing like yourself. But he was quiet. He drove and after thanking him for the ride and appeasing any worry by telling him I was going to see friends, that they were waiting for me and my car was shot and all the regular shit, I rested my head against the vibrating window.

I was getting sick and knew Olympia was only a few miles away but that thought wasn't enough and all of a sudden it was too hot and I was sweating and my stomach clenched in pre-diarrhea cramps and I asked him to pull over and he was like what, no we're only a few miles and I told him this is fine, thanks.

I got sick.

I walked the last few miles to downtown.

I'd never been to Olympia. I was downtown and I stopped at a bus stop, looking at the map and searched for a Martin Luther King or Mission or Hope and found the latter and headed off in that direction.

Maybe half a mile later I was in an older part of town, industrial, seemingly having peaked in the seventies with laundromats and bars. I saw a brother standing with his back against a gray building. He wore a cocked Astros hat and we locked eyes and he was all what you need and I said to get right and he was like a tenth? and I said two and he looked over his shoulder like they always do and spit two pencil eraser-sized balloons out of his mouth and handed them to me as I gave him twenty dollars.

I started to walk away and he said you need more cuz there's other ways of getting and I told him to fuck off from over my shoulder.

I knew I should find out where the campus was, Evergreen. I remembered Mrs. Hudson suggesting it to me my junior year. That it would be a good fit. Liberal, in the Pacific Northwest, a good environmental program. I'd asked what makes you think I like the environment? She'd blushed, shrugging off the question, half pointing to my dreads but stopping short. I thought you'd mentioned it, she responded.

It was November and about five o'clock and the sun was hiding behind the Olympics and it was cold in a wet kind of way. I walked to the BP and asked an acne-faced boy for the key and he said it's for customers only and I tilted my head and rolled my eyes and he smiled and said all right.

I got well.

I came to with pounding at the door. Voices, a man's. Hello? Hello? Are you okay? We're coming in.

A large baldheaded man saying Jesus fucking Christ. Sorry.

Get the fuck out of here.

Just leave.

Wayne, call the cops.

I'm going.

Wayne, cops, now.

I pulled my sweatshirt sleeve down and moved slowly towards my pack against the wall. My needle fell from my lap to the floor.

Fucking Christ, the man said, get that shit out of here.

I gathered everything and he stood in the doorway but moved because he was that kind of guy, his not laying his hands on me not out kindness, just fucking scared of the needle in my hand. Junkies and AIDS and that whole thing. I walked out.

⋮

I didn't know where campus was but I saw a hill maybe a mile away and walked in that direction. The going was slow and pleasurable. The mist or light rain wasn't cold anymore. It surprised me, being that high. I guess I was still a snob that way, thinking the China in Colorado was so much better than the stomped-on tar out west, but I hadn't nodded off like that since Maddie got me high for the first time. Us, sitting in his little Toyota, me crying because it had been three months of nothing, no contact, letters or calls and locked up in some state-run facility, drug court and all, and he showed up at my door and my mom was all get the fuck out of here, you're not ruining her life again and I ran and hugged him and he pressed his hands to the side of my face, really my head, pressing our foreheads together like the pressure was the only thing good enough. And him pulling off into the strip mall three miles from my mom's. I was crying watching him and kept asking questions like when did you get out and whose car is this and he was focused boiling a chunk of tar in a spoon and I was like what the fuck are you doing and he smiled, still with his eyes on the dope, tearing a piece of cloth from the bottom of his T-shirt and putting it over the spoon and sucking the liquid he just boiled through the cloth into a syringe.

Maddie, what the fuck?

But really I didn't care, not really anyway. I was so happy to see him.

Do it to me.

What?

That. Do me.

Really?

I nodded. He kissed me and it was the first time since he got popped at Red Rocks selling to an undercover and he kissed me like he always had and it was our sophomore year when things were smoking buds listening to Phish losing my virginity and it was us running away senior year to go on tour and selling enough Molly to live off of and us dancing with our eyes closed wishing things would always be that good.

It stung.

Maddie kissed the trickle of blood from my arm.

Then it was the slowest motherfucking orgasm like God was making love to me.

I was right about campus being on top of the hill. It was sleepy with its massive evergreens and concrete architecture and kids walking in pairs or alone under the artificial humming of evenly spaced lights. I found a pay phone in the student center and used the one calling card I'd stolen in Bellingham that I hadn't sold. I pulled out my notebook to see which kids from tour lived in Olympia and there were none, none of the real tour kids who did this shit as their lives rather than something to do while in school. I decided to call Tibbs in Arcadia, needing to make my way down south for the rock and gem tour in a month anyway.

Tibbs, what's up? It's Summer.

Yeah.

Yeah?

What's up?

Hey, I need work.

Not over the phone.

Please, I'm hard up like a motherfuck and—

Not over the phone.

And like I could do whatever, man, like trimming or burying stalks or—

I don't know who you are and have no idea what you're talking about.

Tibbs.

Wrong number.

Fuck, Tibbs, I just need—

He hung up.

I slammed the phone down. That's how they all were after Maddie got popped for the second time. Like they were so fucking sure he talked and it was bullshit because Sean pushed kilos of Molly across the country and it could have been any number of reasons his shit was raided because he was stupid like that, gaudy and careless and it wasn't Maddie who talked. And I wasn't Maddie.

I went to the bathroom. I changed my underwear, using a wet paper towel to clean up. I splashed water on my face, avoiding myself in the mirror while drying.

I walked around the student center looking for kids with long hair and patchworks. Kids with baggy cargos, bootlegged Phish shirts and cocked baseball hats. Nothing. I headed toward the library. I walked around and saw a boy reading at a table alone. He wore a Grateful Dead shirt, store-bought. His brown hair hung around his shoulder. I knew he wasn't a tour kid, that this was a hobby for him and he was younger than me probably by a year or two, probably twenty or twenty-one, but he looked up and made eyes and I smiled and walked over towards his table. He looked over his shoulder, like I couldn't really be giving him that smile, that I couldn't really be walking to talk to him. I smiled again and motioned to the chair toward the end of the table and he said yeah, totally, by all means.

Summer.

Justin.

Nice to meet you, Justin.

Yeah, you too.

What are you reading?

What, oh, just some philosophy homework. Plato.

Interesting?

Not really.

I moved a chair closer.

Let me see it.

I pretended to read the pages and rolled my eyes. Jesus, I said.

Yeah, it's not too fun.

I smiled at him. I slowly tucked a dread behind my left ear.

You in school here? he asked.

No, no, taking some time off. Just passing through on my way to Arizona.

Right on.

Yeah. I bit my bottom lip, letting it slide out slowly.

So what are you doing on campus? he asked.

The couple I was going to stay with are having a nasty fight and I had to get out of there.'

Sucks.

Yeah, for sure. So I came up here looking for something to do, kids that wanted to party.

I raised my eyebrows in his direction.

Yeah?

You wouldn't know anyone like that, would you, Justin?

He laughed and leaned back in his chair and they were easy like that, all of the college boys. Like I fit some sort of fantasy for them, a girl in distress stumbling into their lives, a girl with a large backpack and dreads who did drugs and you could see their minds work, all of them the same, the little vision of getting high with me and fucking me and sending me on my way the next morning.

Well, yeah, I mean, I think there's a party tonight, he said.

Yeah? I looked down, then back at him. I said I'm pretty beat from traveling all day, I was kind of hoping just to take it easy, and *party* party, you know? Like just chill and get my head straight.

He smiled. You could come over and hang out for a bit, if you want?

That'd be rad, man, that really would.

⋮

Justin lived on campus. It wasn't a dorm room, more like a little four-person townhouse, but obviously owned by the school. It was decorated with all the usual shit. Dead tapestries, pictures of Bob Marley smoking a giant spliff. A bong rested on the wooden coffee table. I asked if it was cool to shower, just to get freshened up after spending all day on the road.

I locked the door. Nothing in the medicine cabinet. I showered. I felt embarrassed that my vagina was as hairy as it was, then felt annoyed at my embarrassment. I dressed in a cleaner pair of jeans, no underwear, and a thin V-neck long underwear top of Maddie's, no bra. I undid all but the last clasp.

Justin sat on the worn couch. He'd put a Phish show on his computer. I could tell it was something from the '13 tour because of the looping of Trey's guitar. I set my pack down and sat next to him, pulling my legs underneath me. He put his arm along the spine of the couch and then brought it back to his lap.

You want to smoke?

Sure, I said.

I hated smoking. The shit made me paranoid and gave me a headache. He passed me the already-packed bong. I looked at the bowl, seeing it was shitty BC buds and thought of Maddie saying he wouldn't smoke anything that didn't come out of Humboldt and wasn't from hand-blown glass and I held a plastic bong bought from some head-shop and took a hit and Justin cleared the slide for me, which I thought was sweet in a way.

Good, right?

I nodded.

He took a hit.

Back to me.

Back to him.

The concert playing from his computer was definitely from the '13 summer tour. It was Red Rocks, the first night. Maddie got popped two nights later.

Back to me.

Justin filled another bowl and I was annoyed imagining him thinking he needed to get me high enough to fuck him. Like this was his plan.

I was still pretty well from the gas station so the weed didn't bother me. It was almost pleasurable. I looked at Justin. His little scruffy beard that probably had taken months to grow. His curly hair. His eyes were blue, which I thought was pretty.

Back to him.

Back to me.

Back to him.

I leaned forward, my elbow resting on his leg as I pulled the computer over to look at the screen.

I knew it was the first night at Red Rocks.

Were you there?

Yeah.

I leaned back, letting my hand drift from the computer across his legs to my lap.

You're so lucky, he said.

Yeah, it was a rad show.

Back to me.

Back to him.

I've only seen them four times, he said.

I gave him a motherly pout.

It sucks they're on hiatus, like once I get to college, they go off and quit.

I nodded, thinking he was right. Not about him, because I didn't give a fuck. But for us, the tour kids, the kids who gave up everything to make that our life, to follow the band around from city to city, to make our livings selling drugs to kids like Justin, college kids who thought they were down, cutting loose once or twice a year with a hit of molecular ecstasy and thinking they were so rad. It was bullshit, kids like Justin coming into our world a show at a time, their claiming they were like us and it was all good because it wasn't, being homeless following a band around the country, because the music quits being good and the people don't care about anything besides dope and who's pushing what and they throw you out the minute you get popped, like they did to me because of Maddie. And kids like Justin complaining they can't see Phish anymore like it's some big fucking travesty. When really it's a travesty for us because it means we aren't tour kids anymore, nomadic vagabonds but at least with some sense of purpose, but are now just homeless junkies.

I leaned forward like I was looking at the computer screen. I knew my tits were visible through the loose shirt, probably my nipples too. I could feel Justin's eyes on them. I let him look.

I'm so high, I said, giving him the green light.

Yeah.

I playfully pushed him on the shoulder, saying that was some good shit.

I let my hand run down his arm.

His eyes were still on my tits.

I leaned forward so I was a few inches from his face. I looked down at his hard-on pressing against his pants.

What was your intention getting me this high?

I, nothing, I...

I kissed him on the lips. Then again. I leaned back with my bottom lip between my teeth. He put his stupid bong down and brought his right hand to my face. I moved it to my tits. I straddled him. I kissed him and his hands got greedy and soon my shirt was off and he sucked my nipples and I pulled out his dick and it was bigger than I would have guessed and I put it in my mouth and cupped his balls and he was all oh my fucking God that feels good and I listened to the concert trying to remember that night and it would have been us stage right with Tibbs and Caitlyn and Rae and Sean and all the kids, all of us having fun and it being new, Maddie and me in love like nothing and our first summer after running away and us being good kids then, just eating Molly and smoking and chewing Xanax and when the jams got dark and heavy and I knew Maddie would be in a dark place, his retreat into his head and guilt and shame and reliving everything horrible from his childhood, I would wrap my arms around his shirtless waist and squeeze and he'd turn and press his forehead to mine, expel his demons with the pressure of my simply being there. But I couldn't remember that night, not particularly.

Baby, yes, yes.

And I was seeing Maddie at Red Rocks, torso pushed over the hood of a car, some dready narc slamming his head down.

I put my finger in Justin's asshole to speed the whole thing   up.

One gram of heroin. Five counts of drug paraphernalia (two syringes, a

charred spoon, a tourniquet, a bottle of distilled water). Six grams of MDMA. A digital scale. Felony possession and felony intent to distribute.

Oh God, baby.

Pled guilty to four felonies. A maximum of twenty years. He was only doing two.

Justin came in my mouth.

Maddie must have talked, that's why Sean got raided and was serving fifteen to twenty.

I swallowed, because that's what Justin's fantasy called for.

⋮

Justin woke me up in the middle of the night by running his hands over my stomach. He pressed his hard dick between my butt cheeks. He put his finger inside me and I wasn't wet in the slightest and it was too rough. I pretended to be asleep. He put another finger inside me. I told him to put on a rubber. He did. He fucked me from behind and I hated him for that.

I got up early. Justin groaned but his eyes were closed. I took the wallet from his crumpled pants on the floor. His breathing heavy, me taking his computer, his DVDs. His weed. A jar of peanut butter.

I bought three hundred dollars' worth of calling cards at a gas station with Justin's debit card. I threw his wallet in the trash.

I walked back to Hope Street and got five hundred dollars from an Italian-looking man at the pawnshop for his MacBook and DVDs. I waited at the bus stop across from where I'd copped the day before. The same brother came out a half hour later and he was all I knew you'd be back smiling like he was going to fuck me and I told him I had calling cards and he was like ain't no fucking dime and trade and I said fuck man and he said take that shit to a city, you see nuf niggers round here needing to make calls and I said what about you and he laughed and said I do my business face to face and I said come on man and he looked me up and down and said fine, ten to one and I told him no fucking way.

Then get the fuck out my face little girl.

Fine. Let me get a half and he looked around and slipped five balloons out from between his lips and gums and I gave him the three hundred in calling cards and twenty dollars.

Or we could work something else out.

Fuck you.

You know you want it, his lips parting into a smile I knew too well.

Where's the NEP?

Ain't no motherfucking exchange here worth goin' to.

Where is it?

Cops patrol that shit night and day.

Around here?

Got rigs if you need.

Still packaged?

Yup.

I followed him behind the bar to the employee parking lot and he reached behind the dumpster and pulled out a paper bag. He gave me a syringe in a Ziploc bag.

I laughed, asking what the fuck was that?

You want it or not?

That's not sealed.

It's clean.

I shook my head, knowing I needed a new rig because mine broke when it fell from my lap the day before, but I didn't trust anything not in a factory sealed package. That much Maddie had instilled in me, him saying it goes from having a habit to being a junkie the minute you start using dirty needles.

No, I'm straight.

I went to the laundromat a few blocks down. I used the bathroom. The head of my needle was completely fucked, broken and blunt. I put it into my arm and it hurt like a motherfuck and bled onto the white linoleum floor. I couldn't get it into my vein and knew that even if I did the point was blunt and fat enough to rupture the shit and an abscessed vein was an easy way to get dead or at least hospitalized. I boiled half a hit more and loaded it and pulled my pants down and took a booster in my right butt cheek, annoyed I would be having to use almost twice as much to get half as high going through muscle instead of blood.

I sat down.

My vagina ached from Justin and then it didn't as my eyes became weighted.

I passed on a ride from two Mexicans about the same age as me and they yelled at me in a language I didn't understand, pointing to their arms, their faces, their race, but really I thought it was because they were mad they couldn't double-team me underneath some evergreens off of a dirt road. A young family picked me up in a new VW Euro Van and I sat in the back with two kids who were playing guess the constellation with flash cards and I laughed to myself. It was warm and the bumps were rhythmic and I fell asleep.

I woke up to the little blonde girl tapping me on the leg saying we're here, sleepy head.

I smiled at her. She was cute, probably five-years-old with a missing tooth and long stringy hair.

I thanked them for the ride and the father said, for sure, it's no problem, so this is Port Townsend and you can catch the ferry right here in downtown which brings you over to Seattle. He gave me a five-dollar bill and said this should cover it and I said no, don't worry about it I'm good and he said take it, Happy Thanksgiving and be safe.

My look must have given away I hadn't remembered.

Yeah, tomorrow is Thanksgiving, he said.

Why don't you spend it with us? the mother asked.

No, that's really okay.

Come on, we have an extra bedroom and it will be nice, the father said.

I thought about the five us sitting down, them and their kids and turkey and drinks and polite laughs and a clean bed and not having to fuck him for a roof.

That's really kind of you guys, but I am meeting some friends in Seattle and already have plans.

You sure?

Yeah, thanks though.

Here, take this, the mother said reaching into her purse. She handed over a few twenties.

No, you guys have been more than generous, I'm fine, thanks though.

Take it, please.

Thank you.

Be safe.

Thank you.

Port Townsend was a quiet little town, a main street along the ocean with art galleries and coffee shops. I sat down by a fountain at the heart of the four-block downtown. I watched families walk with little kids. Scrubby boat-builder type guys in their Carharrts and beards. Women in skirts. They all seemed to know each other, each person coming across another group exchanging words or hugs, stopping to converse for a few laugh-filled moments. I imagined being one of them. If I traded my pack for a purse, me walking around hugging and laughing as the sun shone over the Puget Sound in my backyard. I imagined walking to work, maybe at a restaurant, waiting tables or maybe cooking in the back, a few of us listening to classic rock or some shit, sweating and bumping into one another but with a warmth that grew from routine and proximity, familiarity, us getting high together after work. And that's what it would be, just me smoking, kicking dope and settling down, paying for a small apartment, selling just enough pot to smoke for free, socially, nothing more. And maybe one of these guys becoming something more to me than an exchanged hug. Maybe we would meet at a small local's bar and he'd tell me his name and buy me a drink and he'd say he built canoes and it didn't pay too well but he got to work for himself and with his hands and do what he loved doing. Maybe it would go slow, his courting me. Maybe we'd run into each other a few times over the course of a month, at the bar, at the coffee shop, on the street and he'd finally be like I just have to ask you if you would ever do me the honor of gracing me with your presence for dinner sometime and I'd blush and say yes, I think I would like that, and he'd cook for me, something simple but elegant like salmon and we'd go to the movies and he'd buy me popcorn and candy and we'd hold hands and kiss like teenagers before going home alone.

And maybe after a year or two I'd have my shit together and be happy and I'd call my mother and say Mom, I want to invite you out to visit.

And maybe Maddie would get out and be clean and want to stay that way and he'd come live with me and it would be like it used to be, us in love.

I took the ferry to Seattle.

⋮

I headed on foot to the western side of Pike. I knew my way around that city well enough from spending time there before and after shows at the Gorge before Shoreline to know that's where you copped so the Sally and needle exchange would be nearby too. As the buildings changed from Starbucks and boutiques to bars and small Chinese take-outs, I looked at who walked around. Seattle was a junkie city, from runaways to motherfuckers who'd been doing the shit since Vietnam. It made me sad, seeing them huddled together talking. Sitting against boarded-up storefronts, a mangy dog lying next to them. Like *real* junkies. People who did whatever it took to get well. Like real motherfuckers sucking dick and scraping res from stumbled-upon spoons into glass stems left over from the crack heads.

I found the Salvation Army and it must have been close to four because the line stretched around the side of the ugly brick building. I scanned the line. Mostly middle-aged white guys and that didn't sit well because if a Sally is full of blacks, drugs are almost always to blame and you are left alone, but if it's white guys then it's a grab bag of everything and some of them are crazy motherfuckers who will pin you down and rape your shit.

Or maybe I was feeling spoiled, over five hundred dollars on me. More than I'd had over the last two months. Maybe I just wanted to sleep in a motel. It was stupid, I knew, spending money like that just because I had it, but I knew the dicks in the Sally would search my bag and even though I'd have the dope in my panties, that didn't necessarily mean it was safe.

I singled out a young girl, probably my age. She was one of those gutter punk kids but was cute enough. She stood in line with what I assumed was her boyfriend.

Hey sister, where's the exchange?

Three blocks down on 3rd, she said, rubbing her nose.

Thanks.

You holding?

Just enough to get right.

Because I'm hard up and if you could just kick me—

Yeah, like half a hit is all, I'm sorry.

I'm talking like just enough to like stave this shit off for a fucking hour...

Can't help you, I said, shrugging and I started to walk away.

Walk away from me bitch, she yelled.

I kept going. People in line looked at her and then back to the sidewalk.

Fucking cunt, she yelled.

A block up I saw the two of them in a reflection of a storefront window. They were walking quickly, maybe half a block behind me. I knew they'd knock me the fuck out and steal my bag and would be savvy enough to reach in my underwear for my money and dope and I started walking faster, thinking about the small knife I had but that was in my pack and I thought about running but the boy would be faster and I thought about turning around and being like fine, fuck, here, take it, because really, it was only like three hits and I had plenty of money to get more and it wasn't worth getting my head bashed in and pack stolen but I just walked faster.

Half a block up I stole a glance from over my shoulder and they had stopped, weren't looking in my direction at all. They talked with another kid on the street. Probably trying to get well, I thought. Nobody is going to the Sally without enough to last them through the night. I slowed down and walked toward the exchange.

It was at the end of the block. No sign or anything other than "Third Avenue Needle Exchange Program" on the glass door. I stepped in. It was like all the rest, a tiny waiting room, maybe five-by-seven with chairs and a receptionist at the end. It was empty, as expected, because late afternoon is a time when junkies are almost always high or doing shit to get there. I walked toward the large black lady behind the window.

Hi, I said.

Afternoon, she said. She took off her glasses and let them hang around her neck.

Name?

I haven't been here.

Take a seat then.

I sat down. I hated exchanges. They reminded me of methadone clinics and I thought of being in Ashville for the 2014 winter and Maddie and I trying to kick but that shit failed as soon as we tried, us waiting a day and staying in that shitty motel and diarrhea and we weren't even sick yet, not really, but as soon as that thought crosses your mind, you're fucked, you're sick, and you need to get well. His probation officer gave him a three-month grace period at the clinic and it was every morning at seven thirty waiting against the wall with ten or so other kids and it was one pill and another after four and it was a horrible time, living there in the mountains of North Carolina. Maddie had to get a job and the only place that hired him was McDonald's and he smelled like fried body odor at all times. I broke down Molly and pushed a few grams a week at the college in town but it was barely enough to pay for the motel and it was us trying to get by like everyone else, up and out the door by seven to get our morning dose and then Maddie to work and me to campus and at night we watched TV and fought because we didn't know what else to do.

All right, come on back, hun.

The woman let me in the side door. She motioned to a seat next to hers. She put her glasses back on, looking at a sheet of paper.

Name?

Jane Smith.

Address?

Just traveling.

Date of birth?

1-1-95.

Blood type?

A-positive.

How long have you been using intravenously?

It's for a friend.

Is this friend a daily user?

No.

Does this friend know about infectious blood borne pathogens?

Yes.

And sexually transmitted diseases?

Yes.

Does this friend want any literature on how to apply for a Rule 25, state funding for rehabilitation?

No.

A list of kitchens or boarding?

No.

The woman put her pen down, the glasses too.

Needle, she said, turning around in her chair to a safe. She spun the lock and I took my needle out from my sock and placed it on the desk. She placed a sterile rig on her desk on the opposite side of me. She looked at my needle.

Your friend didn't try to use this, did she?

No.

Because a head like this will rupture a vein.

I nodded.

The woman intercepted my gaze, which was on the new needle. She sighed. You know, there's a way out, hun.

I nodded.

I was just like you, a tough girl, ain't nobody tell me nothing.

Okay.

You ever think about it?

Yeah, all the time.

⋮

I stayed at an Econo Lodge two blocks up. It was sixty-seven dollars and I knew it was stupid but I couldn't do it, head up to hipster Capital Hill and go to a bar and find some guy to buy me drinks and laugh at his jokes and let him rub my pussy underneath the bar counter before going home and sucking his dick.

Girls were already working in the small parking lot and it was that kind of place, hourly rates and girls getting fucked for a hit of rock. I locked my door and put the one chair against the handle. I ran a bath. I'd bought two more hits from a brother fifty yards from the NEP and I boiled a tenth and got high even though I didn't need to.

That night I lay in bed watching TV. I watched *Friends*. It'd been a long time since I'd seen the show and Ross was being an idiot and I drifted in and out and didn't laugh, thinking of junior high, how even then I couldn't stand the bullshit cookie cutter existence of white Colorado suburbia. I woke up an hour or two later and I watched *Charlie Brown's Thanksgiving*.

I decided to buy a bus ticket to Flagstaff the next morning. It wasn't my thing, the rock and gem circuit, old hippies and peace and love bullshit traveling around the southwest selling chunks of amethyst, but it was better than this.

I shot up again.

Snoopy cooked a turkey.

Maddie talked.

A whore next door faked an orgasm.

I was just like you, a tough girl, ain't nobody tell me nothing.

I used my stolen calling card to call my mom back in Colorado. She picked up on the second ring.

Hello.

I thought about Maddie coming to my door, my mom yelling, me crying, our foreheads touching.

Hello?

The smelly kid with the blanket and fleas eating pumpkin pie.

Dancing, our sweaty heads pressing and pressing and the dark of night like life could never be this good, like please make it stop.

Summer, is that you?

Fuck me nigger, fuck me, from next-door.

Summer, oh my God, where are you?

There's a way out.

Summer baby, please talk to me.

I hung up. I walked to the window. I drew back the curtains. I could see the Catholic Charity with its big twenty foot cross. Some of its lights were burning out and flashed in epileptic bursts through the rain that had descended on Seattle.

Notes From a Dragon Slayer

A dragon slayer is a worthy profession. It's hard and heroic and most of the time you have to do it alone and that can be boring but it's like what Mrs. Parker's always telling me, Netta Mae gonna be nothing but long days and lonely nights flying up out of here. I've seen movies about dragon slayers. They always wear old clothes like potato sacks and then they put on shiny metal and they ride horses and use big long spears that I know are called lances. You have to hit the dragon in its secret spot which is normally in the bellybutton or maybe sometimes the eyes. When you get back people always cheer and the dragon slayer gets the princess but since I'm a girl maybe I'll just get treasure and people's respect.

Mom doesn't know I'm a dragon slayer.

I tried telling Jesse but he just said shut up there's no such thing as dragons and I said yes-hun and he said get out of my way. He's stupid. He's five years older almost thirteen and thinks he's so cool because he has new hairs in his armpits that smell like fajitas. Like he would know if there were dragons or not. He doesn't know about dragons. He doesn't know about me. Like the fact I can run all the way from our apartment to school in less than ten minutes and that's faster than the bus and faster than he could even dream of. Or how I can sneak in and out of my bedroom window at night without anybody knowing not even Mom who never sleeps anymore anyway. Or how I collect things. That's another thing dragon slayers do. You have to carry around a brown bag that's really called a satchel that goes over your shoulder like a purse but it's not a purse because it's a *satchel* and not as girly. You have to take items called artifacts that will help you in your quest. These can be like potions or weapons or even like glittery things that maybe could distract the dragon while you sneak up behind it and even though I said the secret spots were the belly and eyes sometimes it can be the tail. My satchel came from Randy who was my mom's boyfriend before Kevin. The last time I ever saw him he slammed the door so hard the window cracked but just a little. Randy left his brown satchel. I snuck it to my room. It was full of used bits of tin foil like maybe he ate a hundred Hersey Kisses a day. It's not big enough for a lance but it has all my other inventory which is what you call your supplies when you're in the business of hunting dragons which I obviously am.

I've seen plenty of dragons but kind of from the corner of my eye like when Kevin opens my door and I don't move because I don't want him to know I'm awake but I can still tell he's there. That's how it is with dragons. As big as they are they hide really good. I was telling this to Mrs. Parker the other day. We sat on her couch. It's covered in plastic wrap like Jesse's mattress because he wets the bed even though he's *so old* with his armpit hair. Whenever she's not babysitting kids across the street in the nice part of town she's sitting on that very couch. We watched *Wheel of Fortune* which she says is good for me to watch because it's about spelling. Mrs. Parker knows about my chosen vocation of dragon slaying so she asked how it was going. I told her it was going okay but not that great because I couldn't ever get a good glimpse of one. Then she said Netta

Mae the devil dresses in human flesh and I told her I wasn't hunting the devil and she laughed her old laugh that I think is beautiful like a doorbell to a new house. She said evil is evil and I told her maybe she was right.

I felt like this might've been the biggest break yet. Imagine dragons disguised as humans all day except maybe at night when they go out and do dragon things like burn down villages and steal little girls from their rooms. The more I thought about it the more it made sense. I asked Mrs. Parker how I would know if a person was a dragon. She blinked her eyes then opened them real wide so they were like two big white plates sunk into her wrinkly brown face. She said them demons can't hide the look in their eyes.

⋮

I obviously don't have a horse but my bike is kind of like one and even though it's Jesse's and is big and boring blue it works and I call it Temple. A temple is a place where you go to pray before you go on your voyage to kill a dragon. You could say Temple is my best friend besides maybe Mrs. Parker but she's old but Temple's a horse so yeah Temple is probably my best friend.

Kids at school don't like me. They call me stupid and smelly which is fine by me because they don't know what's important in life. All they care about is new things. The girls in my grade always show off their new clothes to make people jealous. I don't care two licks about new clothes although maybe if I weren't a dragon slayer but a princess I would. I'm smarter than every other kid in the third grade. Mrs. Parker tells me this is probably the reason kids don't like me because they're intimidated. Fine by me. I do all my work before I even get home and I spend my free time going around looking for treasures or artifacts for my inventory and of course keeping my eye out for dragons.

Today at recess I found a weapon. It was kind of like a dagger which is what we call a knife in the business. It was orange plastic and when you pushed up on this little lever a blade came out. It was in the janitor's closet. Kids aren't supposed to ever go in there but Mr. Turner sometimes allows me when he can tell I'm worn down by life. I felt a little bad sticking the dagger in my satchel but it's only borrowing.

I'm supposed to go straight home after school. This is what Mom used to always say but now she doesn't say it as much and really she probably has no idea when I come home because her clock is broken like she thinks bedtime is at three in the afternoon or some days not at all. Plus being home is boring. Mom's always yelling at Kevin and he's yelling back and if Jesse is home he monopoly's the TV so I just sit in my room and pretend I'm invisible.

So after school today Temple and I headed toward past the nice homes of Stapleton and way out to the old part of Denver which is actually Commerce City. This is where I had the second great thing of the day happen to me. I was by the Three Seasons where they bring fries and malts out to your car. I was riding Temple around by the dumpsters when I saw a sheet of paper floating around. I thought this was weird because it wasn't even that windy like maybe it was a sign like Mrs. Parker is always saying. I dismounted Temple. I moved real fast and grabbed it out of the air. And lo and behold it was a map.

Other than a horse and a lance and a satchel a map is the most important artifact a dragon slayer can have in her inventory. This sheet of paper didn't have lines or X's but it was directions which I could read just fine because I'm not stupid. I knew the first street on the list and I thought I knew the second one too. But the last turn I'd never heard of. I thought this must be at the far end of town by the trailers which Mom says is a kind of trash we'll never be. But people is people is people like Mrs. Parker always says.

I figured I could make it there and back before it got dark like real dark with only stars for lights even though I had a small keychain flashlight in my inventory. Onward Temple! I rode real fast on the side of 47th. Cars drove by and one even honked because I was kind of in the road because I didn't want Temple to lose her footing in the slippery gravel. I held the map in my mouth which you do when you're a dragon slayer. I sweated real bad and dirt stuck to my skin. I thought about the dragon at the end of the map and then about my dagger maybe not being enough and then about treasure and people liking me and then even my mom waiting for me at home with that big smile she used to do and maybe she'd even make me a rhubarb pie.

I made my first turn on Elm like the map said to. The sun was like a giant marble over the trees and I had to squint to keep from going blind. I figured I'd probably traveled a hundred miles because my legs were burning and that only happens when I travel great distances. I didn't recognize any of the houses and then the houses weren't houses but trailers and I know trailers are houses but not really because they can move.

I turned left on Oak. A man walked by wearing overalls with no shirt and it looked like he needed a bra which I'll need next year when I'm a woman in the fourth grade. He said lost little girl and I was about to tell him yes but I didn't because he was grinning like bad people do when they're trying to act good. This man spooked Temple which is what happens when a horse gets scared and since horses have better tuition than humans I got a little worried too. Right then and there I knew Mrs. Parker was right about dragons hiding in human disguise.

I finally found Q which is a strange name for a street because it's not a flower or tree or even a number. I turned right. Then the pavement ended and Temple was running across dirt. I felt nervous all over my body. The map said my destination was Q17. I slowed Temple to a trot and then to a walk and then I realized I needed to dismount from her because that's what you do when you're real close to a dragon's lair. I opened up my satchel and took out my little flashlight that I pretend is a torch. I took out my dagger too. You never can be too certain.

Q17 was the last trailer next to a metal fence next to the forest and I figured this made sense because the dragon could slip into the forest and go kill people without ever being spotted. There was light shining through the window and the door too. I felt terrified like when my mom and Kevin are really fighting like when they haven't slept in days and things start crashing around and I am in bed deciding if I should slip out the window or not. Mrs. Parker says you can close your eyes and count to ten and breathe real deep when this happens. She says you think good thoughts like about sunshine and love and Saturday morning cartoons and say to yourself this too shall pass. I did that standing outside of the dragon's lair.

Courage is doing things even though you're scared and it's of utmost importance that a dragon slayer have plenty of it. Sometimes I don't. That's the God's honest truth. I thought about every great dragon slayer having to show his courage and then I told myself I was a wimp and then I climbed the three metal steps leading to the lair. I could see legs sitting on a couch. They were pretty legs like real long and white and this secretly made me happy because it wasn't a scaly dragon. I pressed my face to the screen so I could get a better look and then somebody screamed from inside and then I screamed and I told myself to run but my feet were stuck in glue. I closed my eyes and started counting. The door opened. I looked up to see a pretty woman in the shortest shorts like maybe they were for a kid.

She said you scared the crap out of me what are you doing are you lost what unit you live at?

It's like I forgot how to talk. I held my dagger and torch. The map was still in my mouth and this was what the lady took. She read it over and then looked at me. She was pretty with dark hair in knotted snakes and her skin looked like the 2% milk I drink for lunch everyday at school to make my bones strong.

Where'd you get this?

Found it.

Where?

Thee Seasons.

So why'd you come here?

I shrugged. I slipped my dagger into my satchel because she didn't seem like a threat. The lady asked if I lived in the trailers and I said no I live in the Spruce Street Apartments and she asked if I biked here and I said yes and she nodded like this was impressive. She asked if my mom knew I was here. I thought this might be a trick question that adults do so I said maybe and she laughed and told me to come in. I know you're not supposed to go into a stranger's house when you're a kid or even talk to them for that matter but when you're a dragon slayer you have to break certain rules that will help you on your quest.

The inside of her trailer was orange and kind of messy with clothes and a few soda cans and there was a couch and a TV and a little tiny kitchen and that was about it. She gave me a Coke. You can never be too careful when dealing with people on your journey like maybe there could be poison or sleeping powder in the Coke so I pretended to take a big drink but really I just made the swallowing sound.

She said what's your name and I said Netta Mae and she said that's pretty my name's Summer and I said that's pretty too. She said so why'd you follow the directions to my house?

I shrugged and said I thought it was a map to something else.

Like what?

I studied Summer. She was pretty for sure and her eyes were clear and Mrs. Parker didn't say what color dragon eyes were only that you'd know. I didn't know so that probably meant she was an ally which is what you call a friend in dragon speak.

A dragon.

Yeah?

It's kind of my thing.

Dragons?

I'm a dragon slayer. Netta Mae the Dragon Slayer. I found the map and figured it would help me on my quest. But you're not a dragon.

No, don't think so at least. Sorry to disappoint you. I gave those directions to my friend Maddie who works as a cook at the Three Seasons.

Oh.

Sorry hun.

Is Maddie a dragon?

Summer laughed and shook her head and said he's a bunch of things but don't think a dragon is one of 'em.

I fake sipped my Coke again. She asked if I wanted her to call my mom and I shook my head and said there was no need she wouldn't answer anyway and then Summer got this concerned look on her face like I was a kitty or something. She said listen I've been there Netta Mae like right there in the exact same spot believe me. She put her hand on my shoulder. I thought about good touch bad touch but hers was friendly like when somebody scrapes her knee and you get them to stop crying and then I realized I was about to cry and I felt embarrassed and not very full of courage at all.

I said I don't get it. Mrs. Parker always says everything in the world happens for a reason. I found the map and it brought me here but you're not a dragon or even a dragon slayer so what gives?

Summer laughed. It was a different kind of beautiful than Mrs. Parker's like maybe the theme song from a movie. She said maybe I'm supposed to help you on your quest?

How?

Advice?

I rolled my eyes.

She laughed some more and then I did and I accidently snorted like a pig and this got Summer really laughing hard. She stood up like she was looking for something. I asked what she was looking for. She said something to help you on your journey. I started looking around and then I saw a pink bra crumpled by the side of the TV. I pointed. She laughed. I could feel my cheeks burning up. Summer picked up the bra. It was so grownup with pink and white lace. She said why do you want this? I said because next year the girls have to wear bras. It says so in the school booklet because we're women then.

This one might be a little big.

I shrugged. I knew my mom would forget to take me shopping for school clothes and for bras and then I'd be the only girl in class without one and that'd be one more thing kids would make fun of me for. I said never mind it was a stupid idea.

Summer sat next to me on the orange couch. She placed the bra in my hand. It was softer than baby hair. She said if you think this will help then by all means take it. It's yours. My pleasure.

Thank you.

I remember being your age and thinking it would be that hard forever. But it isn't. It gets better. You'll realize your parents don't have shit on you and they're just as messed up as anyone else. But it's not your fault. Nothing you did. You understand?

I nodded even though I didn't.

Because you're a good kid. A good *dragon slayer.* And you'll find what you're looking for. Probably in the last place you look. It just might take a while.

Okay.

Come on I'll give you a ride home.

⋮

There's a piece of armor in the dragon slayer profession that's called the breastplate and it goes across your chest. It took me a few days to realize that's actually what Summer had given me. I wear it under my clothes because it protects my heart and everybody knows your heart is kind of your secret spot like the belly or eyes or sometimes tail of a dragon. The armor is too big so I put a little balled up toilet paper in each side so it fits better and offers more protection. Needless to say, I feel safer and a touch older wearing my new armor.

But that's not important.

What's important is everything that happened today. It was pretty much the weirdest day I've ever experienced even weirder than when we went to Goodwill and I hid in a huge basket of shoes and fell asleep and woke up to some robot voice saying Netta Mae Wilkins report to the front counter.

The weirdness started at school. People have been making fun of me all week calling me boobs and other dumb things so when I was called to Principle Horn's office I figured it was to rat somebody out which I would never do because that's pretty much a no-no being a dragon slayer. But when I got to Principle Horn's office he wasn't there. There was a lady dressed all fancy in a skirt and jacket like a man's and her nails were long but weren't even red or pink just plain colored with white at the tips. Her hair looked like a doll's hair that'd been combed way too many times. I gave a quick glance at her eyes and they didn't seem mean which is to say dragon-like but you can never be too certain.

She told me her name was Hailey which I figured was her first lie because adults who ask to be called by their first names are usually liars. She said she had a few questions for me about my home life. She said there's no right or wrong answers here. You just answer as truthfully as possible. Nobody's getting in trouble.

I nodded. I'm not an idiot and know that if somebody says nobody's getting in trouble they mean exactly the opposite. Lie number two. I looked again at her eyes to make sure I hadn't misjudged them earlier. They still seemed nice like she really cared about me. She said how are things at home?

Fine.

Are you able to get all of your schoolwork done?

Duh. I never miss a homework assignment not even a single point.

She laughed but it was a fake one coming from her throat instead of her belly. Her breath was bad like rotting meat which might have meant she was a dragon. She asked if I was getting enough sleep and enough to eat.

Yes and yes.

And are you happy?

Sure.

What does happiness look like to you?

Like when Mrs. Parker gets the word before the people on *Wheel of Fortune*. She claps and does this giggle thing and I think that's happiness.

Hailey smiled and made a note in a black book. She said who's Mrs. Parker and I said my neighbor who I hang out with everyday. She's in a three-way tie for best friend with Temple and Summer.

And how old is Mrs. Parker?

Probably like a hundred.

I see. Does your mom know you visit with Mrs. Parker?

I shrugged. I said sometimes but sometimes I just climb out of the window so those times she probably doesn't know.

Why do you climb out of your window?

It was at this moment when I remembered Hailey probably couldn't be trusted. I thought real hard about what I'd already said. I rubbed the leather of my satchel. I reassured myself that if Hailey was a dragon or at least an evil dragon slayer I had my chest plate on and that was better than nothing.

Do you feel unsafe at home?

No.

From your mom? From her friends that come over?

Nope.

Remember there are no wrong answers here. You can be totally honest with me. You won't get anybody in trouble.

Roger dodger.

Have you noticed anything different about your mother?

I thought about the question being too big like it would've been easier to answer if she'd asked is there anything about your mother that's the same. The answer would be no. For some reason I remembered this time when I was pretty much a baby and we went camping at Taylor's Falls. It was Jesse and my mom and me and we had hot dogs that were black on the outside and cold on the inside. I was really scared at night not to mention cold and this was well before I was a dragon slayer or even knew things about courage. My mom brought me into her sleeping bag. She told me what every sound was outside of the tent. The final noise was coming from inside the tent and she said that's either your brother snoring or a bear and I laughed so hard and she kissed my forehead and I felt safe.

I shook my head and told her everything was good.

She gave me a fancy business card with her name and number on it. She told me to call anytime night or day if I felt in danger or even simply felt like talking. I slipped the card into my satchel and told her okay.

⋮

After school I was mounting Temple when a hand grabbed my shoulder. I instantly thought it was a dragon and that my time was up like Mrs. Parker is always saying. But it was only Jesse which is pretty much just as bad. He looked crazy with his hair all messy. He said what'd you say do you have any idea what you did what the hell did you do?

I said don't grab me and don't curse at me and I didn't do nothing.

What'd you say to that lady?

What lady?

Hailey or whatever? Who'd you tell?

Nobody. I didn't do anything. Let go of my arm.

Jesse didn't let go of my arm but instead squeezed harder. It wasn't fair because I wasn't ready for an attack which maybe was my fault because a dragon slayer should always be ready for a sneak attack. He said you must've said something because CPS doesn't come around for no reason so out with it.

I didn't say a word. I talked to her and I said everything was good like mom's the same as ever and things are fine.

But before that?

Before that nothing. I didn't rat on anybody.

Because as bad as you think it is now it would get worse if they took us away.

I didn't really know what he was talking about but he was scared and that's something I never see from Jesse not even when Sheriff Murray came to the door asking about the broken windows at the old candy factory that I know Jesse smashed. I thought about being right that Hailey was a liar. Jesse kept saying things about us turning into orphans and having no home and having to move and I told myself I wouldn't cry but I think I was because he finally let go of my arm and said don't cry like a baby. Keep your stupid mouth shut.

Temple was pretty shook up after talking with Jesse so I let her walk the long way home. I kept telling her it was okay and that Jesse didn't know what he was talking about. Temple kept picturing being moved to a huge scary building with rows and rows of beds with mean kids and nuns hitting her with rulers. Temple felt pretty lousy so I told her we should get busy slaying dragons and this seemed to pick up her spirits.

It's a well-known fact that dragons are like other animals and need water so the lake is an obvious place to hunt. Lake Ilene is pretty much as big as an ocean. There's no way you could swim across the whole thing not even wearing a life jacket.

I told Temple to be real quiet when we entered the thicket which is what you call the forest in my circle. I dismounted and took out my dagger. The trees were both the Christmas ones and the ones that changed colors. It was cold in the shade. I let doubt creep into my mind which is something Mrs. Parker says to never let happen. I doubted I was very much good at slaying dragons. Heck, I'd never even seen one like full on. I thought about not even having a shield to deflect fire. Then I thought about dragons maybe not being real. Jesse said dragons weren't real and of course the kids at school said the same thing. What if I was completely wrong and just an idiot girl who was *stupid* and *smelly* like everyone at school said riding around on my brother's cruddy bike with other peoples' junk in my ugly purse?

I used my dagger that I really knew was for cutting open boxes to slice a tree. This can cause the tree to get a disease but I didn't care. I did it to a few trees while I walked around only kind of looking for dragons that probably weren't real. But that's when I saw something. Right there by the water there was a blue tarp strung up between two trees. There was a little fire pit with no fire. There was a backpack leaning against a tree and some boots and a camouflage folding chair. I could hear noise coming from inside the tarp like a raccoon ripping open bags of trash. But then I heard a man's voice in there too. I pushed the blade out as far as I could. I thought about turning around and getting on Temple which is really just my stupid bike and going home or maybe to Mrs. Parkers and watching TV and eating those hard candies that taste like the air fresheners in the school bathroom. But my tuition was telling me to stay and investigate.

Hello?

Hello yourself the tarp said.

I'm armed.

The tarp laughed and I said I'm serious I'm armed with a dagger. You need to show yourself.

An older man who was probably fifty came out from the tarp. He didn't have a shirt on and his stomach was covered in white hair. He wore a camouflage hat. I held my dagger out in front of me. I said what are you doing here?

What am *I* doing here? What are *you* doing here?

I asked you first.

Fair enough. I live here. He waved his hand around and it was then I noticed he was missing a few of his fingers. I know it's bad to be grossed out with handicapped people but his fingers were like the butts of hotdogs I never eat because they look like bellybuttons.

Do not. Can't live outside.

Do to. *Can* live outside.

He smiled which made his eyes real big like he'd just been sprayed by a cold water gun. He seemed crazy but not bad crazy like a dragon or demon. I know that when you're dealing with a person in the thicket they can try to trick you so I figured I'd quiz him to make sure his story held up. I said if you live out here where do you go to the bathroom?

Anywhere I want. Mostly up there.

Gross.

You asked kid.

I'm not a kid.

Young lady.

I'm not a lady because you have to have a bunch of money and fancy dresses to be a lady and even more gowns to be a princess.

Then what are you?

I tossed the question right back at him to throw him off.

He rubbed his stomach that looked like Santa's face. He said he was a vet and I said I don't see any dogs. He laughed a laugh I had to categorize as genuine. He said the kind of vet that fights other people's wars.

I used dragon slayer lingo and asked if he *mangled* his hand in battle.

Bingo.

I thought real hard about him being a solider. I'm not stupid and know he probably fought in the desert like everybody else but I let myself pretend he was a fellow dragon slayer and this felt good for a minute.

He said you didn't answer my question. What are you? You've got a box cutter there like you're some kind of warrior.

I *was.*

Once you're a warrior, you're always a warrior. As much as you want there's no undoing that. The man wasn't smiling anymore and he seemed like he was sleeping with his eyes open which is a real thing because Jesse does it sometimes. I said I wasn't a warrior anymore because dragons aren't real and how can you always be something that never was?

The man shrugged and sat down in his camping chair which made his belly even bigger. He said that's pretty good logic except for one thing.

Huh?

Dragons *are* real.

Liar.

Liar? Right kid. And I suppose I'm lying to say I lost three fingers from the bite of a dragon?

I walked closer to him while studying his hand. It had some of the same white hair on the back of it which was gross but not as gross as the nubs of his three fingers. He said see right here? Those are teeth marks.

I know a thing or two about dragon bites mostly that they always leave a jagged scar. The scars on his fingers were like a mountain range. He said there's this special kind of dragon over in Iraq. It hides all day and all night. Sometimes for years. And you know the only time it wakes up?

At night?

When you drive over it.

I tried to say something but I was too busy imagining a giant dragon lying real flat under the sand waiting for a car or maybe a school bus.

He said they're the most dangerous ones. The ones you can't see. The small ones. The ones right under your nose the entire time.

How do you slay them?

You don't. You think real hard about how much you love your family no matter how damn mad they make you sometimes. Then you pray to a God you've sworn off fifteen years before. Then you tell yourself what you're doing is for the side of good and then you pray again.

But you *were* doing good because dragons are bad.

Dragons aren't bad or good. They *are*. There's no helping them. There's no hurting them. There's just trying to not get dead.

I was confused and my head suddenly itched real bad from a mosquito bite. I mumbled so what's the point of being a warrior?

He laughed even though nothing was funny. He tossed me the ratty camouflage hat from his head. I instantly knew it was a precious artifact to be added to my inventory. He said what other way than war can a kid dethrone his parents as the most important people in his life?

⋮

That night I was in bed eating strawberry Pop Tarts. I wore my breastplate and new helmet that made me invisible. It was really late like probably midnight but my mom and Kevin were yelling like they were talking across the Grand Canyon. I'd already counted to ten and said this too shall pass like a hundred times but they were still yelling or maybe now screaming. I could hear things starting to break. I heard a bunch of bad words. I counted to ten my hardest and then I heard what sounded like an elephant crashing against the wall and then my door opened and I closed my eyes so hard I saw diamonds.

Netta Mae you okay?

It was Jesse. He snuck into my room and was real careful shutting the door so it didn't make that clicking sound. I used my mini flashlight from my satchel to light him up. He was dressed in jeans and the same black T-shirt he always wore. He said let's get you out of here.

Why?

Just shut up and follow me.

All of a sudden I got super scared like worse than I'd ever been because Jesse was being nice and that never happened. He said don't cry be quiet it will be fine we'll sneak out.

It might've been a mistake but I told him about my secret passageway through my window. He nodded and opened the window and hoisted me up. I said wait my satchel and he said we don't have time for your damn satchel.

Outside it was loud with insects. I was shivering even though it was hot. Jesse told me to go to Mrs. Parker's apartment and not to come out until he came and got me for school the next morning.

I was crying.

He put his hand on my shoulder and said go now it's fine and I said what's going to happen and he said nothing it's fine I love you you'll be okay.

And then I was alone. I walked to Mrs. Parker's door. All the lights were off. I thought about her being sound asleep in the flannel dress she wore at nighttime. Then I thought about knocking and having to explain what was going on and even though she's my best friend other than Temple I didn't think she'd like to be woken up in the middle of the night. Plus I knew she'd call the police and we'd be taken away like Jesse said.

I walked down the steps out toward the street. Something hit my arm and I screamed but it was only a moth. The stars were out but they made me feel small. I thought about walking all the way across town to Summer's trailer. I imagined her being nice and rubbing my shoulders and letting me watch TV and eat chips. Then I thought about heading to the lake through the thicket and finding my fellow dragon slayer who'd have a fire going and at least a can of beans cooking and some funny stories to tell me. I felt a little spooked so I reached for my mini flashlight but my satchel wasn't there. I'd left it on my bed. I was alone and defenseless without even a dagger. Not even Temple was there to keep me company. I thought I heard some groaning like a trash can being dragged across the street or maybe like a dragon waking up. I wondered if our entire apartment would be ruined when I got home. I imagined Jesse finally running away like he was always threatening.

My eyes started to adjust a little bit once I was on the street. There was thicket on either side of me. The groaning noise was getting louder plus like something really big breaking branches and I had goose bumps pretty much like chickenpox. That's when I saw my first dragon. It was a massive shadow right above the tops of the trees. I froze right there in my tracks. I couldn't see if it was red or anything because it was so dark but I could definitely see its shape which was all body and a thin neck like a chicken. I prayed for a lance or a dagger or at least for somebody to be standing next to me. Then I prayed for courage. I took a few more steps. That's when I saw another dragon. This one was even bigger like the size of a building and he was all shadows and probably could blow fire but not fly because of his size. My breath was doing that funny thing like a scratched CD when I inhaled. Another dragon sauntered across the street and everything shook and I imagined him flicking his tail and that's all it would take to squish me like a gnat.

Soon I was surrounded. Dragons walked around sniffing each another. Some of them munched on the tops of trees. They smelled like bait containers full of worms left out in the sun. I remembered what the warrior vet had told me about dragons not being good or evil. They were just trying to not end up dead. This didn't really help and my legs were wet with pee and I scolded myself for being a baby. But maybe he'd been right? The dragons didn't really pay me any mind. They walked around like they were bored waiting for school to start. I let myself think they were beautiful and then wondered why I'd ever wanted to slay them in the first place. It felt like we were the only ones left in town or maybe the whole world. I knew nobody would believe me. The kids at school would tell me I was a smelly stupid liar and I knew Jesse was gone and then I thought about my mom smashing things in the kitchen and she wouldn't even listen to me when I told her.

As soon as I started thinking about my mom the dragons disappeared. They didn't run back into the thicket but disappeared into street lamps and billboards and power lines. I didn't feel afraid only completely alone and maybe a little older. I started back home.

$$\vdots$$

The door to my apartment was wide open when I arrived. I strained real hard to hear any more yelling or smashed dishes but it was quiet. I let myself think about my mom being dead and then about Kevin being gone and my mom happy and then the more real possibility of the house being completely empty. I walked inside. It was pretty dark except for the light from above the stove. There were broken things all over the floor. It was a dragon's lair. My mom sat there at the tiny kitchen table not moving or anything. Smoke curled out of her mouth and nose. It was then I saw my satchel on the table. My dagger was out and so was my flashlight and my map and everything else in my inventory. My mom puffed on her cigarette and picked up something white from the table. I realized it was the card Hailey had given me at school and that it would be bad like I was betraying my mom and I wanted to say something but I just stood there staring.

Is this what you want?

I stayed silent. My mom looked dead with how far her eyes were sunken into her face. Her hair was like a scarecrow.

Is it?

I thought about life before I was a dragon slayer before I even knew Mrs. Parker when it was us three playing at the park or coloring while we watched TV. I thought about Summer in her trailer and how she said everything gets better and I'd find what I was searching for in the last place I looked. My mom's eyes were all the dark part and she started crying but they weren't sad tears but the ones you do when you feel sorry for yourself. There was no doubt in my mind what my mom really was. She said is this what you want is this what you want is this what you want? Smoke curled around her fingers. I realized the dragons outside were nothing but shadows turned to friends to fight off loneliness. The vet said dragons were just trying to not end up dead. Is this what you want is this what you want is this what you want? There'd be no treasure or people cheering or even people at least liking me a little bit if I slayed a dragon. I started counting to ten. My mind was a million things people along my quest had told me: *Is this what you want. This too shall pass. There's no good or evil dragons. Parents are as messed up as anyone else and it's not your fault. What other way than war can a kid dethrone his parents as the most important people in his life?*

I was almost to ten and I was picturing what things would look like when I opened my eyes. There wouldn't be plates broken or a hole in the wall and my mom's face would get softer and fuller like it was before and Jesse would be in the other room complaining about something but in a nice way like he was poking fun. And school would be better like I'd never have to eat in the janitor's closet to avoid being called smelly and fat. And Mrs. Parker wouldn't pray over my safety. And Temple would be real. And so would those dragons out in the thicket. They'd be so real and nice and there wouldn't be the need to be a dragon slayer but a *dragon tamer*. Like maybe once they got to know and trust me they'd let me climb on their backs and after like a hundred days of training I'd tell my dragon to giddy up and fly and then our apartment would be the size of a Lego and school would become a dot and I'd realize Mrs. Parker had been right the whole time about it being long nights and lonely days to fly up out of here.

Someone Amongst Us

A) Someone Amongst Us is a Monster

Somebody put a razorblade in the orange tube slide at Edgecombe Park in Stapleton, Colorado. He or she or they taped it blade-up with a long swatch of Duct Tape. Two of our kids were injured. Little Thurman Johnson received the worst of it—a seven-inch gash from knee-pit to buttock—and he was quoted in the Stapleton Front Porch the next morning as saying, "It [the cut] felt like a gazillion beestings." We couldn't believe somebody would be so cruel. There was a town meeting that night, about a third of our two thousand-person subdivision jammed into the high school gymnasium. We stood against the white brick walls. We shouted things we felt like shouting. It smelled like feet. Most of us had our children there. We suddenly didn't trust the neighborhood girls who normally babysat. Sheriff Murray assured us swift justice would be taken, they had some strong evidence, but please, if anybody knows *anything*, to contact him. To alleviate any misguided blame on either the Lutherans or Catholics, Paster Stinson and Father Clemens lead us in a communal prayer. We only kind of bowed our heads. We scanned the gym. Someone amongst us was a monster.

Theory #1: A Teenage Prank

This was the first theory to gain any traction. Perhaps it was the easiest for us to swallow—a misguided prank, kids thinking something would be funny without calculating the ensuing damages. We talked about pranks we had pulled as kids. We remembered how Jake and Dillon Nelson—twins, big kids, starting left and right tackles (both offensive and defensive)— had walked a heifer up three flights of stairs at the high school. But the next morning, instead of seeing a crane lowering the heifer from the roof, they found a dead cow, a cattle prod hole through its right temple.

Needless to say, we understood sometimes pranks sounded better than they actually were. So, this is what we said. We claimed the razorblade was probably meant as a scare tactic, something that would frighten children and mothers alike. That it was harmless. But then we dropped our tone, shuffling our feet a little bit, because it *wasn't* harmless. We couldn't imagine our own kids with sliced genitalia. Deep down, we understood nobody in his or her right mind would think this would be funny. We vowed to catch the bastard.

And from there, we broke away from the counters of Starbucks or from the heated rooms at Core Power Yoga. We formed smaller groups of two or three. We made our voices as serious as possible. We asked who we thought it was. We looked over shoulders. Our little subdivision felt foreign and violent. We said, "Probably that piece of shit Daniels kid."

Suspect #1: Maddie Daniels

Maddie Daniels was the closest thing our suburb had to a bad kid. Not just a normal boy-being-a-boy, but a kid who drank most days before school (when he went); who'd spent the previous summer at Totem Town for Boys for robbing Pete's Liquors (was caught passed out in the bushes less than three hundred yards away); and his acne, well, it was painful to look at. We liked Suanne Daniels, or rather, we felt bad for her, what with Randy's accident while trying to build a tree house. But really, we didn't feel *that* bad for her, because after all, we'd offered help countless times (casseroles, church-led prayers, barbeque invites), all of which she'd turned down. It made perfect sense her son had turned to crime. Something was wrong with the whole family: first the circular saw accident, then the arrests, then the razorblade in the slide. Some of us muttered *cursed.*

So on Wednesday afternoon, just twenty-four hours after little Thurman Johnson was brutally cut, we left our jobs early. These weren't coordinated plans, simply little pockets of us across the outskirts of Denver knowing things needed to be taken into our own hands. We drove in minivans and Subarus. We drove in packs. We showed up at the Daniels house. It was only a frontier build, so we didn't care about driving up on the lawn. We got out of our cars. We didn't talk about the coincidence that the girls from The St. Julian Resort and Spa showed up in their white Jetta. We understood the need for justice and the power of a communal mind and we stood there, maybe ten of us, not exactly sure what to do.

Jake and Dillon Nelson pounded on the door.

Nobody answered.

They tested the handle, which opened. We filed in. The house looked worse than we remembered—that artificial shade of manufactured darkness from drawn curtains (obviously never shaken outside), a sink full of dishes covered in microwaved shredded cheese, the walls covered with dusty pictures of the three of them, younger, ten years before, husband and wife and grade schooler, fishing poles and smiles and life simple and bound to get better.

One of us shouted for Maddie to come out.

Silence.

Then Jenny from The St. Julian Resort and Spa let out a frustrated sigh and pushed her way through our group and braved the way down a ten-foot hall. She opened a door. The flimsy particleboard ricocheted against the wall (frontier builds were so budget). We stared into filth. We thought about our children turning out this way. About soiled sheets and grease stained comforters and a TV flickering and two liters of Code Red Mountain Dew and fifths of Wild Turkey and we pretended not to see the crumpled socks poking out from underneath the bed (we'd either been there ourselves or had teenage sons). We felt disgusted with Suzanne Daniels and with Randy for being careless with the saw and with ourselves for letting this go on in our suburb. The whole room looked like a crime scene. We told ourselves this could never happen to our families. Then Dillon or Jake Nelson (who can really tell the difference?) held up some sort of marijuana pipe fashioned from a bottle of generic Advil and a trumpet mouthpiece. We stared. It was fastened together with silver duct tape. The almost-empty roll lay next to the pipe. We'd found our monster.

We sped (seven miles over) to the small police station at the edge of Central Park Boulevard. We tumbled out of our cars. Most of us felt jealous of the Nelsons because they held the evidence or maybe proof. Doris looked startled at our entrance. We shouted that Maddie Daniels was the bastard who'd hurt Thurman Johnson. We tried not to stare at the left side of Doris' face, the slack skin an avalanche after her stroke. She told us Maddie Daniels had been picked up for drunken disorderly three days prior. He'd been sitting in County ever since.

And just like that, our shoulders slouched.

We didn't feel smart or brave or much of anything other than confused. We stood there and watched the tail of the Felix the Cat clock swing back and forth. Doris asked if there was anything else she could help us with. We told her no, avoiding the sight of her slack face as we exited the station.

B) Someone Amongst Us is Evil

The next attack occurred on the handrail of Hidden Falls. It was the same setup—a single strip of tape and an outward-facing razorblade—and five-year-old old Laura Feinstein was the one who happened to squeeze the railing for support as she descended the steps. Her mother, Samantha, was a few steps ahead, probably anxious to inspect the slides before her daughter set out to play. Samantha said the sound was animalistic, inhuman. She was smarter than most of us, being

Jewish and East Coast and everything. We puzzled over some of her words in the Stapleton Front Porch—*propensity, indignation*—and although we felt horrible for their family, we secretly felt it was some sort of karma (we can only take so much of being looked down upon).

A second meeting was called.

This time we didn't bother sitting and we shouted real things, demanding answers, some of us lacing our accusations with profanities. Even our children joined in. They understood what was going on. They talked on the playground and they formed their own hypotheses. Little Thurman Johnson, fresh off his stitches, was granted the microphone. He said, "Somebody is evil."

We shook our heads in agreement.

We didn't bother pretending to pray.

Theory #2: A Child-Hater

We started to put it all together. It was obvious Sheriff Murray was worthless (we murmured about the one year left he had before retirement). We thought about the locations of the attacks being parks. We realized parks were monuments to children, and boom, we had our motive: the evil bastard hated children.

At home, we told our kids they needed to play inside. Little League games were cancelled. Youth groups for both the Catholic and Lutheran contingencies were postponed. Even outdoor recess at Stapleton Tech Elementary was rescinded. We quickly grew frustrated with our children, their yelling, their running back and forth in front of the TV (the Rockies had a crucial four game series against Arizona). To compensate, we yelled. We told them to knock it off, to go to their rooms. They begged to go shoot hoops or play One O'Clock the Ghost is Out. We told them to go to bed.

It didn't take long for this to become beyond tiresome. We could only take so much of our own children. So when Hailey Davis, the lone social worker for our privileged suburb, phoned us to explain her theory, we listened. We nodded. We covered the speaking end of the receiver as we hissed at our horribly behaved children. We agreed—yes, Christa Wilkins was definitely the one seeking vengeance upon our town.

Suspect #2: Christa Wilkins

Christa Wilkins wasn't part of Stapleton proper—we knew explicitly that the Lake Ilene Inn where she worked housekeeping in exchange for a room was outside of our borders by forty-nine yards, thus technically Aurora's problem—and it was this fact that allowed us to feel better about our little slice of heaven. She was a regular at Chips, practically having to be pulled out of the bar every night, even after her children were born. We knew enough about methamphetamines from watching *Breaking Bad* to know this was Christa Wilkins' problem. The two arrest reports in the Front Porch confirmed our suspicions. Plus the shorts she wore…no woman not on drugs would allow the bottom-curve of her buttock to be exposed.

So, when two years ago, Hailey Davis and Sheriff Murray showed up at her apartment and proclaimed Christa Wilkins an unfit mother, taking little Netta Mae away to be a ward of the state, her return contingent upon Christa having a year of sobriety (which had yet to happen), we were not surprised. We knew little Netta Mae would be happier with some foster family in Cherry Creek. We knew Christa Wilkins was a junkie, always would be, no doubt.

Standing in our own kitchens cradling the phone, we thought about times our own children had either been disciplined or gossiped about. We thought about the shame, the rising-neck-hair feeling of *how-dare-you?* We thought about what Christa Wilkins must have felt (true, it was deserved in her case, but she wouldn't see it that way). It would be a primal hatred and resentment, one bent on hurting those who she'd perceived to hurt her: our children who filled the streets and parks and slides.

We hung up our phones. We climbed into our cars. We even switched our radios from the Rockies' matinee to the classic rock station.

There were more of us this time.

It wasn't just the men from Allstate and the gals from the spa. Minivans filled our caravan. The Pontiacs of the old. We spotted a few of our children on BMX bikes pedaling furiously. Drew Johnson rode his Segue. Down Central Park Blvd we went, fifty or so cars. This time, we really didn't care about speeding (10 miles over). The Nelson Twins had their windows rolled down and they screamed the lyrics to *Born in the USA* and we realized this was what we all mouthed, the same song on KQRS, and with this communal realization, we changed our silent lip movements to the belting-out of lyrics.

We pulled into The Lake Ilene Inn. It was a single-story motel, red, ten rooms, a gravel parking lot, the centerpiece of the structure a faded Coca-Cola vending machine that only took change. Those of us who couldn't fit in the lot parked in the street. Some of us left our keys in our ignitions. The sun was angry and we were angry and somebody left The Boss playing from his stereo. Hailey Davis led the way. She'd done this once before, two years before. She walked to Room 1. She banged her fist against the red door. We stood there a hundred deep. We yelled for Christa to come out. And then we thought we saw movement, some fluttering of the yellow drape, but before we could yell that we knew she was in there, we heard a shattering of glass. We turned. Little Laura Feinstein stood there with a rock in her bandaged hand. We thought she looked like biblical David (was that story in the shared testament or just ours?). There was another crash. Another and another and another.

Maddie Daniels climbed through the window. We applauded his efforts (we understood he was trying to become a different person, a better person, and we felt like this was mostly due to ourselves). The motel door opened. We heard shouting, a female. We couldn't wait to confront this child-hater. We thought of vigilante justice, razorblades, an eye for an eye. We fought amongst ourselves to gain entrance.

Christa Wilkins sat on a worn futon in place of the standard-issue card table. She looked better than we remembered—decent clothes that covered her legs, washed hair with relatively few split ends, her face clear of the sores we once mistook as acne. Just as we were about to start in with the accusations and demands for her to come clean, we paused. We stared at the ceiling directly over the queen bed. It shined. We studied the source of shine. We realized they were pictures. They were glossy pictures of smiling babies and sleeping babies and burping babies and babies eating Grubbers. They were clipped from magazines. All of them. Hundreds of babies staring down like a glass-bottomed view of Purgatory. We thought about the effect of such a sight—to be watched by that many creatures in need of protection—and we shivered and fell silent.

This collage was proof enough.

Hailey Davis was the first to speak: "How could you?"

Christa feigned bewilderment. This only angered us more. It emboldened us. The Boss drifted in through the broken windows. We didn't realize we were doing it, grabbing Christa, but we were, all of us. We yelled that she was evil and deranged. We used words like *unfit* and *endangerment* (these would sting, we knew). And even though *pedophile* didn't necessarily fit, we called her that too. We held her in place and we thought about our children. We thought of the good times—Scotty Douglass as Joseph in last year's Lutheran tableau service, him forgetting what to say and stopping midsentence and yelling, "Line"; the entire seventh grade softball team making it to state and even though they were dismantled by Colorado Springs, they shook hands and exchanged pins with the other team and were awarded the Denver Sportsmanship Award. This was what she was trying to destroy.

Christa screamed.

We didn't care.

She yelled, "I'm innocent."

Hailey Davis stood on the motel bed. She ripped the perverted collage down. Magazine clippings fell. The wind gusted through the window and they floated, hundreds of smiling babies, and Christa kept begging for mercy, and we said, "Why don't you ask Thurman Johnson or Laura Feinstein about mercy?"

We pinned Christa to the floor. We stared down at a woman we hardly knew. Snot dripped from her nose. Her eyes reminded us of wounded deer (all of us had had those shots that grazed skin or hindquarters).

"Please, you have to believe me," she begged. "I love children. I would do anything for children. Please, stop."

We didn't care.

Bridget from *Bridget's Bleaching* unwrapped a package of razorblades and divvied them out. The Nelson twins each took one. Little Thurman Johnson took one. We told ourselves Christa's tears were fake, were for herself. She kept fighting. We told ourselves we were doing good. The Boss was wrapping up his song, and this felt like a natural climax, all of us bending over the writhing body of a woman who loved drugs more than children, and in turn, wanted to enact her failure onto us. We felt embarrassed at the darkening of Christa's acid washed jeans and pretended not to notice.

Just as little Laura Feinstein was about to slice into Christa's leg, a bullhorn sounded throughout the muggy motel room: "Back away from the woman."

We turned.

Sheriff Murray stood there bald and old in his brown uniform. Sweat glistened off his leathery forehead. He held the bullhorn in one hand, a pistol in the other. Both shook. He said things about this not being the way, that everybody was entitled to her own fair trial, innocent until proven guilty. We parted. He knelt down to Christa Wilkins. She lay there in her own snot and urine. He put her in cuffs. We almost felt bad until we mumbled that Murray had been packing it in all year, just waiting for retirement, and didn't have the stomach for actual justice.

We walked out of the motel. Our cars idled. The sun made the pavement on Central Park look like the deepest of lakes. We climbed into our Foresters and Jettas and bikes and Segue. We peeled glossy magazine clippings from the soles of our shoes. The smiling babies looked nothing like our own. We didn't want to go home to our families and all their silent and not-so-silent demands.

C) Someone Amongst Us is a Terrorist

The third attack occurred at Martin Luther King Park. The perpetrator chose to line the final foot and a half of the third base line with partially buried razorblades. When TJ Prunty (All-Conference his junior year, early murmurings about him being in the running for Mr. Baseball the next season) tried to stretch out a triple, he slid headfirst into home. He let out the loudest scream we'd ever heard. He was cut clear from his left pectoral to the right of his navel.

We didn't hold a meeting at the school.

We didn't need to.

We were all there watching.

Father Clemens yelled that somebody needed to put a stop to this reign of terror. Not wanting to be outdone, Pastor Stinson asked God why our town was being terrorized.

The dirt surrounding home plate was dark and clumping.

Somebody amongst us was a terrorist.

Theory #3: Terrorism

We felt stupid for being so slow. How could we not have seen it? It wasn't a teenage prank and it wasn't a spiteful mother. Hell, it wasn't even really about children; it was an attack against our peace of mind. Against our feelings of safety. An attack on our quiet lives and the status quo and the smiles we gave each other and the missionary sex that filled our bedrooms on Saturday nights. It was against city and state parks. It was against baseball. It was against America.

We listed the foreigners in our town. We shouted it was the Vangs. This nomination was quickly dispelled by know-it-all Samantha Feinstein (supposedly they were "Hmong", who had helped us in The Vietnam War). Probably those goddamn Lopezes, one of us yelled. No, their oldest son was fighting in Afghanistan. The Smiths! They were from Mississippi and were just black, not foreign.

And then we all realized it was the Feghahaties.

Suspect #3: The Feghahaties

We knew the Feghahaties were from *over there.* Nobody knew exactly which hellhole of a sandbox country in particular, but what did it matter? The skin and nose and the bushy eyebrows and the last name—what non-terrorist has that many h's in a name? It made so much sense. They'd shown up three years ago. They didn't have kids (guilty), didn't go to either the Lutheran or Catholic church (guilty), his first name was Hesam (how close was that to Hussein?) (guilty), and although they seemed like a nice enough couple and Hesam had singlehandedly brought a least a million dollars to Stapleton through the employment of a fracking crew out past Blue Mound, it didn't matter; in fact, as we noted, this over-emphasis on assimilation was a little suspicious (guilty).

We held baseball bats. The Nelson twins tore apart the chain link fence, passing out sections of piping. Kids grabbed rocks. Bridget staked her knuckles with acupuncture needles. Maddie Daniels held some sort of glass bong. Samantha Feinstein held a sun umbrella. Sheriff Murray un-holstered his Glock. We didn't even need to get into our practical modes of transportation; the Feghahaties lived nearby, just down by the lake in the nicest house Stapleton had ever seen.

We started down Central Park. It was hundreds of us, each and every second growing. We felt like those brave souls hoisting the flag on Iwo Jima and maybe like firefighters with soot coving their faces on 9/11. People driving to Starbucks pulled over and jumped out of their cars, armed with windshield scrapers and glowing cigarette lighters. Our whole suburb. Our wives and children and neighbors we wished would actually mow to the three-quarter inch ordinance, all of us a swelling mob, hardly able to fit on two lanes of pavement. We would restore our town to how it'd once been. We would restore our open doors and unlatched windows and our children's playtime at the local parks and we'd restore our sense of freedom—that's what this was really about—and maybe it was about the paling of the communal shade of our Norwegian skin and the restoration of our most pressing argument: to take weekly communion or not.

The Feghahaties' house stood there like a big *fuck you.* It was three stories and had more windows than TCF bank on 4th Ave. The giant flowerpots at the front door were gaudy and tasteless. Somebody said *sheik money* and we didn't know what that really meant, but had heard it on Fox News, and we rolled with it—*take your goddamn sheik terrorist money and leave.*

Sheriff Murray rang the doorbell. We listened to an ascending melody ricochet throughout a too-big home. We thought about the shrill buzzing in our own houses.

The door opened.

Hasem stood there in a smart button-down and brown slacks. His smile faded as he saw our numbers. We all were silent. We heard the accented voice of his wife and then she was there and her face went through the same flattening. We knew they knew. They didn't protest. Their silence was an admission of guilt. We inched closer. We all inched closer. An entire suburb climbed onto a terraced entrance and we told ourselves this was what was needed to save our children and ourselves and our town and country.

And before one of us took the first swing, we all had the same memory of moving into our new homes. Some of these homes we'd constructed from the ground-up, some of them were purchased once the lives of the previous owners fell apart through boredom and alcohol and affairs. We'd been happy then. Happy because even though our yards were tiny, they had fences. Happy because there were four community pools with a strictly enforced *residents only* edict. Happy because we'd fled the suburbs of our youth, cutting our teeth on the gentrified grit of city living, before realizing we wanted green grass and elementary schools with iPads for every student, before we realized we wanted a recreation of our own childhoods, safety and homogony of socio-economic class of paramount importance. We remembered the hope we'd felt then. How our wives had made seven trips to Sherman Williams before finally getting the hue of purple for the nursery correct. How our husbands had sat on the deck, grills sizzling, that sly grin, followed by a family pleasing *I think we're ready to finally get that golden retriever.* We remembered the hope of things only continuing to get better. Or maybe it wasn't hope, but a feeling, a certainty—us paying our dues with student loans at third-rate institutions of higher learning, us struggling through setting up LinkedIn profiles and our first positive chlamydia tests and a miscarriage or two and our jealousies at vacations of acquaintances on Instagram and apartments into condos into duplexes—that we were one move away from being able to relax and reap the rewards of being born Caucasian and Christian (the Feinsteins obviously were doing just fine) and upper-middle class, which, we knew, our homes in Stapleton would allow us to do. We remembered our first nights in our homes. We remembered reading to our children, trying to play up the excitement of change rather than its terrifying nature. We remembered making love to our spouses (wasn't even a Saturday). We remembered walking through our new homes, pausing in each room as we turned off the lights, feeling lucky or blessed, but maybe more like we were finally being rewarded for all of our oh-so backbreaking hard work. But standing on the Feghahaties' gaudy front steps and seeing their faces go through various levels of comprehension, we remembered our own moments of reckoning when we realized that Stapleton would not, in fact, fill the role of our convenient-to-lean-on God and deliver us from Evil. Maybe this was when we walked into our beautiful homes and saw our spouses pounding flesh with neighbors or during The Great Recession or when we reached perfection through game or fitting into a zero or when we understood our children were not our own or when we learned to squelch the crushing meaninglessness of everything through inebriation or when we first felt others' capacity for cruelty or when a simple grazing of a penis shattered every conception we had of ourselves or when the revenge we thirsted for was really love or when the monsters we feared were our mothers and fathers and spouses and children. Or maybe it was our first nights in Stapleton. Maybe after we turned off all of the lights, we made our way to the master bedroom. Maybe we weren't tired so we masturbated in the shower. Maybe we slipped into bed. Maybe we turned on the TV, the volume at three. Maybe sleep wasn't coming. Maybe we thought about this being from excitement at our new homes in our new subdivision, excitement at our new lives. And maybe, just maybe, we were able to push aside the realizations that we were still the same people we'd always been and had pretended not to be; there wasn't a single thing we could do to protect our families from the world's ability to spit out people who were ruled by the fear of not getting something they wanted or losing something they had. Maybe we were able to do that, maybe.

We don't know who swung first, only that we all did, trying to restore the belief that fear and loss and blame were containable emotions.

V. Joshua Adams, Scott Shibuya Brown, Brian Rivka Clifton, Brittney Corrigan, Jessica Cuello, Barbara Cully, Alison Cundiff, Suzanne Frischkorn, Victoria Garza, Reginald Gibbons, D.C. Gonzales-Prieto, Neil de la Flor, Joachim Glage, Caroline Goodwin, Kathryn Kruse, Meagan Lehr, Brigitte Lewis, Jean McGarry, D.K. McCutchen, Jenny Magnus, Rita Mookerjee, Mamie Morgan, Karen Rigby, cin salach, Jo Salas, Maureen Seaton, Kristine Snodgrass, Cornelia Maude Spelman, Peter Stenson, Melissa Studdard, Curious Theatre, Gemini Wahhaj, Megan Weiler, David Wesley Williams

jacklegpress.org